**"What's** [...]

Cassidy l[...]

Tim prete[...] [...]t nails and her purple-tipped ones. "It's me touching you, something I wanted to do all evening."

She didn't smile or shoot back some pithy remark guaranteed to make him grin. Instead, she pulled her hand from his.

"You don't have to do this, you know," she said softly, her expression serious.

"Do what? Be nice?"

"Pretend to be interested in me." Cassidy stopped at the edge of the driveway and faced him. "While I appreciate it, we both know you're only hanging with me now because of the bun."

Tim cocked his head. Sometimes it was as if she spoke a foreign language.

"In the oven," Cassidy patted her flat belly.

He almost grinned but pulled the smile back at the last second.

Her blue eyes were so serious and there was an uncharacteristic frown between her brows. He also saw fatigue and weariness in the way her shoulders, normally so straight, drooped.

He raised his hand and cupped her cheek. "I'm with you because I like you."

\* \* \*

**Rx FOR LOVE: Just following doctor's orders...**

Dear Reader,

Have you ever met a person who is quirky, charismatic and a whole lot of fun? That woman is Cassidy Kaye. She's become a successful business owner *in spite* of her upbringing. But who to pair her with was the question.

Tim Duggan has been hanging around in the background since the first book in the Rx for Love series. I've always thought of Tim as a good man in desperate need of some sparkle in his life. When Cassidy came on the scene several books ago, I knew the two would be perfect for each other.

One story within this story was how I came up with the name Esther for one of the hero's twins. It's such an old-fashioned name, isn't it? Years ago, when I worked as a hospice RN, I took care of an elderly patient named Esther. One night when I was sitting with her, she told me she'd been named after Grover Cleveland's daughter Esther. She was a lovely woman, and I've never forgotten that bit of trivia. I decided to bring the name back in this book in the memory of both Esther Cleveland and the Esther I once knew...

I enjoyed writing Tim and Cassidy's story. I hope you enjoy reading it!

*Cindy Kirk*

# The M.D.'s Unexpected Family

———

## Cindy Kirk

**HARLEQUIN**® SPECIAL EDITION®

Recycling programs
for this product may
not exist in your area.

ISBN-13: 978-0-373-65897-8

The M.D.'s Unexpected Family

Copyright © 2015 by Cynthia Rutledge

**Printed in U.S.A.**

From the time she was a little girl, **Cindy Kirk** thought everyone made up different endings to books, movies and television shows. Instead of counting sheep at night, she made up stories. She's now had over forty novels published. She enjoys writing emotionally satisfying stories with a little faith and humor tossed in. She encourages readers to connect with her on Facebook and Twitter, @cindykirkauthor, and via her website, cindykirk.com.

### Books by Cindy Kirk

### Harlequin Special Edition

#### *Rx for Love*

*Ready, Set, I Do!*
*The Husband List*
*One Night with the Doctor*
*A Jackson Hole Homecoming*
*The Doctor and Mrs. Right*
*His Valentine Bride*
*The Doctor's Not-So-Little Secret*
*Jackson Hole Valentine*
*If the Ring Fits*
*The Christmas Proposition*
*In Love with John Doe*

#### *The Fortunes of Texas: Cowboy Country*

*Fortune's Little Heartbreaker*

#### *The Fortunes of Texas: Welcome to Horseback Hollow*

*A Sweetheart for Jude Fortune*

#### *The Fortunes of Texas: Southern Invasion*

*Expecting Fortune's Heir*

Visit the Author Profile page at Harlequin.com for more titles.

To Sia Huff for suggesting I name
the black-and-white kitten Domino.
It fit him perfectly!! Thanks, Sia!!

## Chapter One

Cassidy Kaye knew the instant Tim Duggan walked into the Green Room. Though she was busy doing hair for those participating in the Jackson Hole Bachelor/Bachelorette Auction, her spidey senses never failed to alert her whenever the handsome doctor was nearby.

Out of the corner of her eye, she saw him pause in the doorway, a tall man with a thatch of hair the color of mahogany. His hair was cut stylishly short above a face with a strong jaw and straight nose. His hazel eyes looked green at the moment, but she knew they could turn a mesmerizing golden brown in a heartbeat. He was boyishly handsome, down to the sprig of freckles across the bridge of his nose.

His gaze scanned the room, his expression solemn.

When she'd first heard Tim would be filling in for his friend Liam Gallagher, she'd been stunned and disbelieving. Unlike the other bachelors up for bid this evening, Tim was a family man, a widower with twin seven-year-old daughters. He certainly wasn't a party animal. Other than escorting librarian Jayne Connors to a few social events now and then, he didn't even date.

When his gaze settled on her, something that looked almost like relief lifted his lips and she felt warm all over.

"Back in five," she told Zippy Rogers, a young woman whose thick dark hair practically begged to be placed into a sexy twist.

Cassidy wove her way through the small area just off the main ballroom of Spring Gulch Country Club, loving the energy in the air. With each step closer to Tim a different kind of excitement filled her. Embracing the sensation, she sidled up to him.

"Hi." Cassidy cursed the odd breathlessness that attacked her whenever he was near. To compensate she offered him a cheeky grin. "Word on the street is you're up for bid on the meat market tonight."

He winced.

She could almost see his mind spinning like a hamster wheel as he attempted to come up with the proper response to her not-so-proper comment.

"Liam had an allergic reaction." He shifted from one foot to the other. "Right now his face is puffed up like the Incredible Hulk."

Liam, an all-around nice guy, was a child psychologist who'd recently returned to Jackson Hole to set up practice. Cassidy felt a stirring of sympathy. "Poor guy."

"He hated to back out at the last minute."

"If he resembles the Hulk, it was a wise move," Cassidy said matter-of-factly. "For these events, handsome, not hulk, is what brings in the money."

Tim's gaze lingered for a moment on the pretty blondes, sensual brunettes and one dazzling redhead getting their hair and makeup done. It slid to the group of young men standing together talking.

Other than Liam-the-absent, the guys on the chopping

block tonight weren't his buds. These men were business-men and ski industry people, at least five or six years younger than Tim. His social circle—and hers—was composed primarily of medical professionals and young entrepreneurs with a few attorneys and social workers tossed into the mix.

Cassidy fell into the entrepreneur bucket. She owned a successful hair salon—Clippity Do Dah—in downtown Jackson. In the past year she'd expanded into doing hair, nails and makeup for events, such as weddings and other special occasions.

"I'm not sure exactly what I'm supposed to do." Tim shoved his hands into his pockets and rocked back on his heels. "Liam just told me to show up."

"Lexi Delacourt is coordinating tonight's fund-raiser. You know Lexi."

"Of course." The lines of strain on Tim's face eased.

Lexi was a mutual friend. She was also as classy and elegant as they came. The pretty social worker brought that class and elegance to anything she touched, which meant the auction wouldn't be sleazy. Or at least as non-sleazy as bidding on another human being could be.

"I'll take you to her." Cassidy looped her arm through his, congratulating herself on so quickly finding a reason to touch him.

As always, being this close sent blood coursing through her veins like warm honey. Though Cassidy normally preferred bright colors and flash, Tim's brown trousers and cream-colored shirt suited her just fine. In fact, on him she found the subdued colors incredibly sexy.

Cassidy glanced down, wondering if he liked her bright orange skirt that resembled a tutu—complete with tulle—topped by a clingy lime tee. The outfit was one of her faves.

"This way." Cassidy tugged on his arm.

His feet remained firmly planted. "You're busy. I don't want to interrupt."

Cassidy looked at him blankly.

Tim gestured toward Zippy, who was busily applying another layer of color to her mouth.

Cassidy approved of the young woman's efforts. After all, could lips ever be too red?

"No worries." She tugged again, more firmly this time, and he moved with her, the faint intoxicating scent of his cologne teasing her nostrils. "Zippy is the last woman up, so I have plenty of time."

He nodded. "I just didn't want to disturb you."

She smiled to herself. What would he say if she told him everything about *him* disturbed *her*, but in only the very best of ways? Cassidy barely resisted the urge to ask. Instead, she steered the conversation in another direction. "How are Esi and Elle?"

Tim cocked his head and stared as if she'd spoken a language he hadn't yet mastered.

"Oh, you mean Esther and Ellyn." Warmth filled his eyes the way it always did whenever he spoke of his daughters. "They're well. Spending the evening with Grandma and Grandpa."

"I bet your mother had a coronary when she heard you were filling in for Liam tonight."

Cassidy didn't have to be a fly on the wall to know how that discussion had gone down. Suzanne Duggan, retired schoolteacher, helicopter grandmother and all-around pain in the butt would never approve of her doctor son participating in anything as gauche as a bachelor auction, even if it was for a good cause.

"She didn't say much."

Tim may have kept his tone offhand but Cassidy wasn't fooled. Mama bear had definitely given him a few hard swipes of her tongue.

"What did Jayne think?" This time it was *her* tone that was carefully neutral. To complete the trifecta, she paired the voice with an interested expression and a slightly raised brow.

"Jayne?"

"Jayne Connors," Cassidy prompted.

"I didn't think to mention it."

Relief surged, as sweet as a bottle of cold beer on a hot summer day. Obviously Tim and Jayne were still casual, though Cass had to wonder for how much longer. It was hard to miss the desire in the librarian's eye whenever her gaze landed on him. Not-so-plain Jayne clearly had Dr. Duggan in her crosshairs.

"…for such a good cause."

Cassidy realized that while her mind was tripping down the plain-Jayne path, Tim had been speaking. Thankfully, thinking on her feet was a specialty of hers. After all, as a hairdresser, she spent a lot of time on her feet.

"Raising money for the new Women and Children's Center is something I fully support," he continued. Compassion filled those hazel eyes. His caring nature was one more check in his positive column. "For such an affluent community we have so many women and children who struggle…"

For a second, her throat constricted and breathing came hard. Instead of remaining stuffed away in a rarely opened file cabinet in her head, the comment brought her own childhood front-and-square.

Cassidy plucked the disturbing memories from her head, shoved them back into the file cabinet and firmly shut the drawer. The past had no place in her life. She was all about the present and the future.

"Lexi is right there." Cassidy gestured with her free hand, wishing the auction registration desk had been farther away. She wasn't ready to release Tim back into the world. These one-on-one times were rare and the warmth of his skin beneath her fingers an unexpected pleasure.

"I should speak with Lexi." Yet he made no move to step away.

Though Cassidy sometimes wondered how she could be the only one to feel the sizzle that was so blatant whenever they stood close, she wasn't foolish enough to entertain the thought that Tim hesitated because he wanted to spend a few more moments with her. He was simply uneasy about what he'd agreed to do and was trying to put off beginning the process for as long as possible.

"I have this image of standing up there and not getting a single bid." He emitted a slightly embarrassed chuckle. "I'm a middle-aged dad. Who's going to bid on me?"

Tim wasn't fishing for a compliment; he wasn't that kind of guy. He obviously had no idea just how appealing he was to the opposite sex.

"You're thirty-four. You're successful. You're hot."

He laughed. "Yeah, right."

"If it will ease your mind, I'll start the bidding," she promised him. "Kick things off."

Gratitude flooded his face. "You'd do that for me?"

"Hey." She punched him in the shoulder. "We're buddies."

Okay, perhaps that was a stretch, but saying it felt incredibly good.

"You're a very nice person." His gaze lingered on her face so long that her lips began to tingle. For a second, she had this crazy thought he might kiss her.

Instead he squeezed her shoulder and strolled off in Lexi's direction.

After Cassidy finished making Zippy even more stunning, she took a few moments to touch up her own makeup and hair.

The auction of five women and five men had already started. The order had been predetermined beginning with a female and following a female–male format. Liam, or rather Tim, would be last on the auction block.

From the laughter and applause that arose from the ballroom each time the bidding concluded for an individual, Cassidy decided it wouldn't take long to get to Tim.

Still, she lingered in front of the long mirror, taking a second to add a touch more orange-marmalade gloss to her mouth before fluffing her hair with her fingers. For the evening festivities, she'd resurrected the true blond of her childhood then tipped the ends with royal blue to match the color of her eyes.

Though she often wore glasses in vivid hues or patterns, the frames were a fashion accessory rather than a necessity. Tonight she'd left them in the small apartment over her shop, the place she now called home.

Cassidy smiled broadly, making sure there were no lipstick smudges on her teeth. Satisfied, she sauntered into the ballroom on five-inch heels.

After obtaining a number for bidding, she secured a spot halfway back from the stage and watched the spirited bidding for a date with Zippy. Mr. Business Exec with the receding hairline and Mr. Snowboarder with the sun-streaked shaggy hair both seemed equally determined to win a date with the beautiful attorney.

Zippy was the last woman on the list. The bidding reached one thousand dollars before Business Exec conceded to Snowboarder. Once the applause ended, many of those who'd stayed to watch headed to the adjacent ballroom where silent-auction items flanked the perimeter of the room and a champagne fountain anchored the center. A plethora of hot hors d'oeuvres were dispensed by waiters in black pants and white shirts, holding silver trays.

Thankfully, not everyone left in search of food and

drink. Cassidy calculated at least a hundred remained in the ballroom when Lexi stepped forward to introduce Tim. The dark-haired social worker, lovely in navy chiffon, included in her introductory remarks that Tim had grown up in Jackson Hole, was a respected member of the medical community and the father of twin girls.

The young doctor's face remained calm but Cassidy wasn't fooled. He was nowhere as relaxed and confident as he appeared. Her fingers tightened on the numbered paddle in her hand. She'd made a promise and was ready to do her duty.

Nick, Lexi's husband and well-known family law attorney, was serving as the event's guest auctioneer. He took the microphone from his wife and his gaze scanned the audience. "Do I hear a bid of one hundred?"

For a second the room was silent. One hundred was the lowest acceptable bid. From what she'd overheard while she waited, the lowest winning bid so far had been three hundred, while eleven hundred was the night's record. Most had come in around five hundred.

Cassidy was just lifting her paddle when she saw a redhead off to her right raise hers.

She recognized the woman in the sexy black dress that hugged a taut body and emphasized ample breasts. Leila Daltry was a customer at Clippity Do Dah. She stopped by regularly to get her hair cut and for an occasional color boost. A registered nurse, the striking redhead worked in the obstetrics department at the hospital. Though she wasn't the right woman for Tim, Cassidy liked her well enough.

Nick asked for a two-hundred-dollar bid. When none was forthcoming he moved into his going once, twice speech. Cassidy stopped him by lifting her number. No way was she letting Leila get Tim that cheap.

Leila turned slowly and her cat-green eyes narrowed.

Though the RN had always been friendly enough, Cassidy absorbed the feral gleam directed her way and grinned back.

If Leila thought a hostile glance could intimidate her, she was mistaken. Cassidy Kaye ate feral cats for breakfast.

"Three hundred," Nick confirmed when Leila waved her paddle as he upped the bid.

The curious gazes of the well-dressed men and women in the room were now shifting between her and Leila. Once again, Nick upped the bid. Without even thinking, Cassidy lifted her number.

"Four hundred is the bid," Nick called out. "Do I hear five?"

The redhead hesitated now, her gaze shifting from Tim's impassive expression to Cassidy's cool gaze. Though nurses were paid well, the cost of living in Jackson Hole was through the roof. Five hundred dollars was a lot of money.

Leila tossed her head and raised her paddle.

"We're at five hundred dollars," Nick pronounced. "Will someone give us six?"

*Let it go*, Cassidy told herself. Five hundred was a respectable bid.

"Going twice," she heard Nick say.

Without taking a second to talk herself out of it, Cassidy shot her hand into the air.

"We have six hundred."

Leila's head snapped around and the satisfied smirk on her face vanished. If looks could kill, Cassidy would be six feet under.

"Going once, going twice. Six hundred dollars to number ninety-eight."

It was a charitable donation, Cassidy told herself as she

wrote out the check. Though she had to admit dropping that amount of money in a single night hurt.

Or rather it did until she turned and found Tim standing. Right. There.

"I'm sorry you got stuck," he said.

Normally never at a loss of words, for a second Cassidy could only stare. Her heart gave a painful twist.

"I mean, I know you were only trying to increase the bid. I can give you the money to—"

She shot out a hand, stopping him before he could say more. "You're not getting out of our date that easily. I bought you fair and square, mister."

He smiled then, a warm easy lifting of his lips that did strange things to her insides. And when he took her arm, she realized he was worth every penny.

They strolled into the ballroom, where they both enjoyed a glass of champagne. After handing the empty glasses to a passing waiter, they wandered out onto the veranda, where the conversation shifted from mutual friends and future events to their upcoming "date."

"I'll pay for the evening." Tim's tone brooked no argument. "You pick where we go. Fair?"

Cassidy considered for a moment then nodded.

The moon bathed his face in a golden glow and a light breeze tousled his hair. He really was a great-looking guy. Not only did he have a fabulous face, his lips were firm and perfectly sculpted.

As she stared, she wondered what they would feel like, taste like...

"Sounds like we've got a deal." He stuck his hand out but she ignored it, keeping her gaze focused on his lips.

Cassidy firmly believed hesitating or second-guessing was for wimps. Stepping close, she wrapped her hands around his neck and covered his mouth with hers.

## *Chapter Two*

That smoking-hot kiss was still at the forefront of Tim's mind two weeks later when he pulled into his parents' driveway. Probably because this afternoon would be the first time he and Cassidy would be alone together since she'd surprised him so thoroughly after the bachelor auction.

Over the past four years, his friend Jayne had brushed several kisses across his cheek. Nothing that came close to the sensual feel of Cassidy's warm full lips plastered against his mouth. Before he could get his rioting emotions under control, he'd kissed her back. And it had taken all of his willpower not to continue kissing her.

He wondered if that was how they'd end this evening, too...

"Yippee, we're here," one of his daughters called out from the backseat as he eased the car to a stop in front of the two-story white clapboard that had been his home as a child.

Large leafy trees protected the house and the lush green lawn from the late-afternoon sun. A variety of perfectly groomed bushes added to the home's well-tended appearance.

By the time Tim pushed open his car door, the twins had already hopped out and sprinted up the sidewalk to his parents' front porch.

Esther and Ellyn loved spending time with their grandma and grandpa. But this afternoon, Tim had found himself wishing Finley Davis, the teenage daughter of friends, was available. He knew his mother's feelings about this date with Cassidy and he wasn't in the mood to hear her tell him again that Cassidy was clearly out to snare herself a wealthy doctor.

Stepping out of his hybrid SUV, Tim expelled a resigned breath. Suzanne Duggan, retired grade-school teacher and A-plus grandmother, was a wonderful woman. But there was no denying she could be a trifle opinionated.

Thankfully, it wasn't Suzanne, but his father who sauntered around the side of the house just as the screen door slammed shut and the girls disappeared from sight. His father waved a greeting, his gloved hand gripping a wicked-looking pair of garden shears.

Though in his mid-sixties, Steve Duggan could pass for a man ten years younger. The recently retired engineer was tall, topping Tim's six-foot frame by a good three inches. His sandy hair still held the red all three of his children had inherited, although in recent years more and more silver strands had been added to the mix.

Tim met his father's warm hazel eyes and realized, not for the first time, how fortunate he'd been to grow up in a home with two loving, supportive parents. From the moment his daughters had been born, he'd been determined to give them that same experience. Except now, with Caro gone, he had to be both father and mother.

*They need a mother.*

Tim ignored the voice inside his head and the accompanying fear that gripped him, fear that he was somehow shortchanging the girls by choosing to remain single. But his situation was different than most widowers. His practice was challenging. At the end of the day, there was no time left for the demands of a wife. He'd already failed one woman. He wouldn't make that mistake again.

At ease with his decision, Tim gestured with his head toward the shears. "Looks like Mom is keeping you busy."

His father smiled ruefully. "The woman's honey-do projects will keep my free time occupied into the next millennium."

The two men laughed, both aware that was no exaggeration.

As his father fell into step beside him, Tim sensed his curious gaze. Steve paused at the bottom of the porch steps.

"I was surprised when Suz mentioned you'd be dropping off the girls at four. That seems a bit early for a date."

It seemed early to Tim, too. But Cassidy had paid six hundred dollars. Six hours or so of his time didn't seem much to ask.

"Cass has a full evening planned," he told his dad. "Beginning with grabbing some pizza, then checking out Brew Fest."

When Tim had stopped by Cassidy's salon earlier in the week to find out what she had in mind for their "date," she'd asked if he had plans for Old West Days, a popular yearly event held the last Saturday of May. Other than taking the girls to watch the parade in the morning, Tim had been available.

"I'm surprised the woman could take time off today," his mother said in lieu of a greeting as she stepped out onto the porch. Suzanne was a slim, attractive woman with a sleek bob of light brown hair and bright blue eyes. "If you're a beautician, Saturday is a big day."

"It's her salon. I imagine she sets her own schedule." Tim deliberately kept his tone mild, refusing to get drawn into a pointless discussion. He glanced around. "Where'd the twins disappear to?"

Suzanne's tense expression softened at the mention of her "girls." Esther and Ellyn were his parents' only grandchildren. But something told Tim it wouldn't be long before his sister and her husband added to that number.

"The moment they hit the front door they made a bee-line straight for Miss Priss and the kittens."

Tim smiled. "And how is Prissy?"

His parents had reluctantly taken in the calico last year when Silas, an elderly neighbor, had moved to a nursing home. The older gentleman had been panicked at the thought of his best friend going to an animal shelter. He'd assured his neighbors that Miss Priss had not only had all her shots but she'd also been spayed.

Six weeks ago, the supposedly neutered cat had given birth to four kittens.

"Prissy is a sweet girl," Suzanne said with a fond smile. "And an excellent mother."

From his mother, that was indeed high praise.

"Darn cat is spoiled rotten," his dad groused. "Do you know she won't drink from a bowl? Miss Particular will only drink running water from the spigot in the tub."

His father's tone said clearly what he thought of that practice.

"Hush, Steve. From what I've read about cats, it's a primal thing."

Before a parental argument ensued over an animal neither of them had really wanted, Tim changed the subject. "Have you found homes for the babies?"

"For three of them. So far, no takers for the runt," his mother said with a sigh.

Runt was a mischievous male with a black head, a white body and a raccoon-striped tail. An odd combination to be sure.

Steve fixed his gaze on his son. "Your girls adore the runt."

At his father's raised eyebrow and the pointed look that accompanied the comment, Tim lifted his hands, palms out. "One day I'll get them a pet. Now is not the right time."

Tim expected his father to come back with some pithy comment. Instead his expression turned thoughtful. "I've found the best things are often those that are unexpected."

If his father's cryptic remark was intended to make Tim reconsider his decision to punt on kitten number four, the play failed. "I'm not changing my mind."

He slanted a glance at his mother and found her staring.

She gestured toward his jeans and white polo, frowning slightly. "What made you decide to dress so casually for your date?"

Though Suzanne had made it completely clear she thought the whole bachelor-auction-date thing had been a mistake, obviously in her mind that didn't negate the fact that her son had an image to uphold in the community.

"It's Old West Days." Tim glanced down. "And this isn't really a date."

He didn't know why he'd added the last part. Actually, this was as close as he'd come to a date in the four years since Caro had passed away. While he may have escorted Jayne Connors—a media specialist at the local high school—to various functions over the years, that was because he and Jayne had an understanding. They'd agreed to fill in as each others' plus-one when needed.

"You're absolutely right. It's not a date." His mother's lips tipped in approval. "In fact, that's exactly what I told Paula when she called in a panic."

Tim knew Paula was Paula Connors, Suzanne's BFF and Jayne's mother. The women talked every day. When they weren't on the phone, they were texting each other. The two friends belonged to the same clubs, volunteered at the hospital and served together on too many community committees to count.

He'd have thought the women had more important things to discuss than his personal life, which was nonexistent. "Why does Paula care if it's a date or not?"

"Oh, Tim." His mother clucked her tongue. "She cares because of Jayne. You know she and I still hope the two of you will get together."

Tim stifled a groan. He'd walked right into that one. It had been about a year after Caro died that he'd revived his childhood friendship with Jayne. From the start he'd been clear he hadn't been looking for anything more than friendship. Thankfully, Jayne felt the same way. The only ones who couldn't seem to get the message were their respective mothers.

"Jayne and I are friends, Mother." Tim wished he'd recorded those words so he could simply pull out his phone and push Play each time Suzanne put on her matchmaking hat. The thought of how she'd react to that stunt made him grin.

"I'm happy you find this so amusing." Suzanne took a step forward, her compact body rigid and stiff as any soldier. Though only five foot three, she was definitely a force. It was easy to see how she'd been able to keep classes of rowdy fifth graders under control during her years of teaching. "Well, son, let me tell you what I know."

His father shot Tim a sympathetic glance before pivoting on his sneakers and retreating around the side of the house.

"You and Jayne are perfect for each other. She's a good person. While this Cassidy creature—"

"Not. One. More. Word." The steel in Tim's voice brought his mother up short. He didn't want to be a hard-ass, but on this matter, he'd brook no argument. Up to this point, he'd tried to ignore his mother's subtle digs against Cassidy, but he'd had enough. "Cassidy Kaye is a well-respected businesswoman in this community. I won't allow you to disparage her character."

Suzanne blinked. She opened her mouth but when her eyes met his steely ones, she appeared to reconsider and closed it without speaking.

Seizing the blessed moment of silence, Tim changed the subject. "Are you certain keeping the girls overnight isn't a problem? I don't anticipate being out late. I can easily swing by and pick them up."

"No, no." Suzanne waved a dismissive hand, regaining her composure. "They've been looking forward to a sleepover with Grandma and Grandpa."

"Okay, then." He thought about going inside to tell his daughters goodbye, but knew it wasn't necessary. This was their second home. "Thanks again."

Tim was almost to the car when his mother called his name. He turned, cocked a brow.

Suzanne hesitated, chewed on her lip. "I hope you have a wonderful evening."

Tim accepted the olive branch she'd offered with a smile. "I'm sure I will."

Cassidy took a bite of the Philly steak pizza and nearly groaned in ecstasy. "Oh-my-gosh."

Across from her in the booth, Tim grinned and picked up a slice. "That good, huh?"

"Positively sinful. Take a bite. You'll see." She let the flavors linger on her tongue. Even as she savored, she watched Tim from beneath lowered lashes, eager for his reaction.

When she'd asked what kind of pizza he liked, he said anything that didn't have anchovies, while admitting hamburger was a particular favorite.

She'd nearly grimaced, stopping herself in the nick of time. Hamburger pizza? Boring with a capital *B*.

Then she noticed that Perfect Pizza—a popular eatery in downtown Jackson—had added a Philly steak option. She'd immediately known that was the one she wanted them to share on this special night out. He'd been agreeable and it now sat on the table between them, a gooey mass of cheese and perfectly spiced meat.

"Wow." Tim's eyes met hers. "This is good."

She shot him a wink. "Told you."

As he chewed, he glanced around. Following the direction of his gaze, she took in the dining room area. Even though it was only a few minutes past four, the place was packed.

"I can't believe all the people that are here in the middle of the day." His voice reflected the surprise in his eyes.

Cassidy decided the man really needed to get out more. Anyone who ate out with any regularity knew Perfect Pizza was *always* busy. "In an hour it'll be standing room only."

"Good call on coming early." He took a sip of soda. "Are you going to tell me now what's on the agenda for the rest of the evening? Or is that still a secret?"

Cassidy picked up her slice of pizza, her lips slightly curving as she took a bite. Tim was a planner, a busy OB doctor who scheduled his personal life with the same precision he used in his medical practice.

When she'd told him she'd chosen the Saturday of Old West Days for their date, he'd fished for a detailed outline of the evening. She'd deliberately been vague, hoping the uncertainty would keep his thoughts on the evening... and on her.

Of course, she had no illusions anything would develop

between them. They were from two different worlds. Even back in high school, she'd known her crush on him would go nowhere. Guys like him didn't date girls like her.

The pizza caught for a moment in her throat before she determinedly swallowed it down. Only one thing mattered. Tonight, he was hers and they would have fun. She'd make sure of it.

"Cassidy."

Startled, she blinked away thoughts of her past and looked up to find him staring. At her. More specifically, at her bright pink lips.

Her heart played hopscotch in her chest as Tim leaned forward, reaching out to her, carefully avoiding the pizza that sat between them.

Cassidy held her breath.

"You have a piece of—" the side of his finger brushed her mouth and sent heat shooting through her blood "—cheese."

She gave a shaky laugh. "Guess you can't take me anywhere."

He smiled, but there was a strange heat in his eyes. Or perhaps she'd simply imagined it, because a second later it had vanished. "You look lovely tonight."

"Thank you. I wanted to do something in honor of Old West Days." Though Cassidy loved flashy dresses and short skirts, for today's festivities she'd chosen a pair of jeggings that hugged her long, slender legs like a second skin. She'd topped the tight pants with a bandanna tee in lime green. A bright blue belt cinched the shirt tight around her waist. Cowboy boots completed the ensemble.

Though she'd momentarily considered pulling her hair up in a stylish tail, at the last second she'd decided to let it tumble loose around her shoulders, better to show off several thin streaks of lime near the front.

Cassidy knew she looked her best. She'd made sure of

it. But she wasn't the only hottie in the room. "Allow me to say, Dr. Duggan, that you look übersexy this evening."

Her gaze lingered on his white polo and sun-bronzed, muscular arms.

Tim laughed a bit self-consciously.

"No lie. Jeans, white shirt and buff bod do it for me every time."

He laughed. "Now it's my turn to thank you. I can't remember the last time anyone told me I was sexy."

"You've obviously been hanging around the wrong women."

He only grinned and moved the conversation to her business, something Cassidy could talk about for hours. In addition to her hair salon, Clippety Do Dah—that happened to be doing a rockin' business—last year she'd expanded into hair, makeup and nails for special events.

"Is Hailey still helping you out?" Tim asked.

Speech therapist Hailey Ferris was a genius with makeup. For the past couple of years she'd been helping Cassidy with special events.

"Not anymore. Too much on her plate. Wife to Winn, mother to Cameron and now being pregnant..." Cassidy lifted her hands and let them drop. "That's not even taking into account her speech therapy clients."

"I forgot that she's part of that multi-therapy clinic Meg Lassiter started," he said, referring to another of their friends.

"Her plate totally runneth over." Cassidy took another bite of pizza. She was happy for Hailey, truly she was, but Cassidy really needed the help. "She told me she'll fill in when I'm desperate, but knowing her situation I won't ask."

"Do you have a replacement in mind?"

She shook her head. "I've been beating the bushes and coming up empty. If you know anyone—"

"I may."

Cassidy vowed if he said Jayne Connors, she was going to slug him. Or throw up. Or maybe both.

"Jewel Lucas."

The slice of pizza hovered an inch from Cassidy's lips as an image of the dark-haired woman with the vivid green eyes came into focus. "I thought she worked for the paper?"

"She does special features, but it's not anywhere near full-time." Tim relaxed against the back of the wooden booth. "I ran into her at the grocery store last week and she mentioned she was looking for another part-time job. Kids are expensive. And she's a single parent."

Jewel had given birth shortly after high school graduation. Supposedly the father could have been any one of a number of guys. The pretty brunette had always marched to the beat of her own drummer. Something she and Cassidy had in common. "What makes you think she's qualified?"

"Caro used to say Jewel had a way with makeup." He looked sheepish. "Forget I said anything."

"No. No. Thank you." Cassidy paused. "How old is her son now?"

"I believe Cullen is in middle school."

Another positive, Cassidy thought. "I'll definitely keep her in mind."

The subject switched again and Tim found himself telling Cassidy little anecdotes about his daughters. To his surprise, her eyes didn't glaze over and she seemed genuinely interested, especially when he got to the part about their fascination with the kittens.

"I always wanted a pet when I was growing up." A shadow passed across Cassidy's pretty face. "There were some feral strays around the neighborhood. I'd feed them when I could. Still, they rarely got tame enough to pet. It's hard to trust when you've been burned."

Silence hung between them for several moments.

"My mother still has an available kitten."

"You should take it," she urged, which wasn't at all the point he'd been trying to make.

He shook his head. "Pets are a lot of work."

Tim couldn't help recalling Caro's long-ago response when he'd once mentioned the possibility of getting a dog or a cat.

"And messy," he added. "I know my mother is always sweeping up hair."

"A little hair on the floor isn't such a big thing." She flashed a smile. "Speaking of hair, you're due for a trim."

"I'll give you a call next week and set something up." Tim hesitated, realizing he wanted to see her again and not just for a haircut.

He wanted to chat with her over dinner about her job and his practice, about kids and pets and mutual friends. He felt comfortable with her. And, as he'd discovered this evening, if he didn't want to talk, she was more than willing to take the conversational ball and run with it.

Should he ask her out for real? The moment the thought crossed his mind he remembered his daughters and the responsibility he carried. There was no way he could toss dating into the mix when his free time was already so limited.

For now, he would enjoy this evening.

Tomorrow was soon enough to return to the real world.

## Chapter Three

"If I get on the bull, you have to get on it, too." Cassidy pinned Tim with her gaze and he heard the challenge in her tone.

After sending their saturated-fat levels into the strato-sphere with the Philly steak pizza, Cassidy suggested they stop at Wally's Place, a popular local saloon, for an after-dinner drink and dessert.

For Caro, the perfect after-dinner drink and dessert had always been a glass of Sauternes and crème brûlée.

For Cassidy, the drink of choice appeared to be Corona straight from the bottle and one of Wally's famous "salted peanut chews." She popped the last bite of the bar into her mouth and slanted another glance in the bull's direction.

A red-faced tourist was slowly pulling himself up from the padded floor next to the mechanical bull.

"There's no line." Cassidy's tone held an excited edge. In one fluid motion she stood and shoved back her chair. "This is our chance."

Seeing no good way out, Tim slowly rose to his feet. "You really want to do this?"

"Do leopards have spots?"

Though he was pretty sure they didn't, he took the response as confirmation. The appealing way her tight-fitting jeans hugged her backside kept his mind occupied as he followed her to the other side of the bar.

"Do you want to go first?" She paused by the bull, slapping one hand on the side, as if staking a claim. "Or can I?"

*Can* I? She spoke as if being first up was something to be prized.

Tim gazed at the mechanical contraption. He'd been in Wally's many times over the years, but had paid little attention to the ride. Right now, the doctor in him couldn't help but think of all the ways Cassidy could get hurt.

If she was determined to do this—and it appeared she was—he would go first. That way she could witness the danger up front and close.

From the time he'd been small, Tim had been a thinker. Unlike his two sisters, he'd never been impulsive. Normally his caution served him well. But this time he hesitated too long. While he was pondering the situation, Cassidy scrambled onto the bull. She now sat, listening intently as the man in charge gave her pointers.

When the operator paused to take a breath, Cassidy slanted a glance in his direction and winked. The impact of the flirtatious gaze had him sucking in a quick breath. For whatever reason, her smile did the craziest things to his insides.

Refocusing on the bull, Cassidy wrapped the reins tightly around one hand. In a surprisingly graceful gesture, she lifted the other hand high in the air.

The operator, a bald guy with a Fu Manchu mustache and an easy smile, dropped a cowboy hat onto her head. "Ready to ride?"

This was wrong. Reckless. Crazy.

Fear sluiced through him. She could be seriously hurt. "Cassidy, don't—"

"Let 'er rip," she called out and immediately the bull began to move slowly up and down.

She made an engaging sight in her tight jeans and the green tee that showed off her curves to full advantage. The cowboy hat perched on her blond curls only added to her charm. Though he recalled vividly how soft she'd felt against him when they'd kissed, Tim saw muscle definition in the arm holding the reins and in the long legs gripping the bull as it picked up speed and began to buck.

A whistle from between the teeth of a gangly cowboy split the air. Within seconds a slew of men gathered around, cheering her on.

Tim was powerless to do anything but watch and admire. The look of pure joy on her face as she and the bull moved as one held him transfixed.

Finally the ride ended. Cassidy emitted a loud whoop and hopped off. After handing the hat back to Fu Manchu, she waved cheerily to her "fans" then sidled up to Tim.

"It's a real kick." Her breath came in excited puffs and her cheeks were an enticing pink. "You're going to love it."

Though Tim seriously doubted that, he wouldn't back out. A deal was a deal.

He strode over to the bull with a confidence he didn't feel, secured the reins and wished—for the first time— he'd at least *tried* rodeo club in high school.

"Don't force it," Cassidy murmured in a low undertone meant for his ears only. "Relax and move with the bull."

Moving with the bull wasn't difficult, not at first. Then, just as Tim thought he might be getting the hang of it, the blasted animal went loco. It shifted side to side before pitching radically forward, nearly sending him toppling.

But he held on and—remembering Cassidy's words—did his best to relax and stay loose.

His heart pounded. Sweat dotted his brow. Adrenaline zipped like a lightning bolt through his veins. Tim heard himself whoop like Cassidy had only minutes before. Holding tight to the reins with one hand, the other sliced the air.

"Ride 'em, cowboy," Cassidy called out.

He grinned as another hard lurch nearly sent him toppling. But he didn't panic—panicking wasn't in his nature—and stayed loose.

It felt as if he'd just gotten into the groove when the bull slowed then stopped. Even before Tim's feet were back on solid ground, he was shocked to find himself wishing the ride had lasted longer.

The thought had barely crossed his mind when Cassidy let out a squeal and flung her arms around his neck. The momentum of her body slamming against his sent him staggering back. Quickly regaining his footing, he swung her around.

When they stopped twirling, he kept his arms around her, his gaze on her laughing face. Mesmerized by Cassidy's luscious hot-pink lips, eyes that almost looked violet in the dim light and the intoxicating, sultry scent of her perfume, he couldn't bring himself to look away.

Seriously tempted to kiss her right then and there, Tim didn't know what to think when she stepped back, grabbed his hand and tugged him straight through the doors of the saloon.

While perplexed, he couldn't help but feel that leaving was a good thing. When she'd first gotten off the bull, he'd noticed how many of the men stared as if she was a piece of meat and they hadn't eaten in a week. No, Tim had zero qualms about leaving the bar.

Finally pausing once they reached the boardwalk, Cassidy grinned up at him. "That was a blast. I had so much fun."

*Was*? *Had*? Immediately picking up on the change in tense, Tim fought a surge of disappointment and forced a light tone. "Are you telling me the date is over?"

For a second she simply stared. Then she wagged a finger at him, blue eyes laughing and a little too bright. "You're not getting off that easy, Doctor. I have an entire night of debauchery planned. Trust me, we're just getting started."

A stagecoach ride couldn't by any stretch of the imagination be considered debauchery. Still, Cassidy had always wanted to check out this Old West Days attraction and this "date" with Tim seemed the perfect opportunity.

"Last year the girls begged me to take them on a stagecoach ride," Tim informed Cassidy as the old-fashioned coach, painted in vivid shades of red and green, creaked its way through town with them inside. "But the line was so long we gave up and got cotton candy instead."

*Cotton candy.*

Cassidy smiled. Something else on her list for tonight. "The rainbow kind is my favorite."

"Then I shall buy you some." His gentlemanly tone reminded her of the guys in the old movies Cassidy watched when she had trouble falling asleep.

She loved this teasing, relaxed side of Tim. Since his wife died, he'd seemed so somber.

One of her goals tonight was to show him how much fun life could be, if you didn't take it—or yourself—too seriously. By the smile on his lips, her plan appeared to be bearing fruit.

Cassidy relaxed against the back of the tufted leather seat, wishing Tim would loosen up even more and put an arm around her shoulders. She could picture the scene now.

Picture herself resting her head against his broad chest, playing with the buttons on his shirt—

Without warning, the stagecoach jerked, propelling Cassidy forward. With the lightning-fast reflexes of a former high school wide receiver, Tim pulled her against his chest as if she was a ball sent his way in a Hail Mary.

"What happened?" She knew her slightly breathless delivery had little to do with the sudden jolt and everything to do with the thrill of having his arms finally around her.

"I'd say we hit a buffalo. Or a rut." He chuckled. "One of the perils of traveling down a dirt road to add authenticity to the ride."

"Oh." Cassidy expelled a shaky breath but didn't move a muscle, afraid if she did he might release her. And that she couldn't abide. Not when she was finally right where she wanted to be.

"You're okay." His tone was soft and soothing, his hand stroking her arm in a gesture that was obviously meant to be reassuring.

Obviously he'd concluded her labored breathing was due to nearly planting her face in the rustic floorboards. The truth was, his nearness, his arms around her, was stoking the fire that had burned in her belly since he'd arrived at her apartment door.

After a moment, he shifted uncomfortably.

Cassidy lifted her gaze and found him staring. From the predatory gleam, she wasn't the only one experiencing the effects of the closeness. Slowly, with her eyes firmly fixed on his face, she moistened her lips with the tip of her tongue.

The deliberate action was calculated to draw his attention to her mouth, a mouth that yearned for a long, slow taste of his lips.

By the flash of heat in his eyes, the ploy worked. The

web of attraction that had been hovering dropped and tightened around them, shutting out the world.

Though the road had turned smooth as a baby's backside, instead of releasing her, Tim tightened his hold. Which was just fine with her.

Cassidy reveled in the closeness and the spicy scent of his cologne. Her entire body tingled with anticipation.

Tim leaned close and cupped her face gently in one large palm. The lips she wanted so desperately on hers were only a breath away.

Placing her hand flat against his chest, Cassidy smiled up at him. She prayed he'd see in her eyes she wanted this as much as he did, maybe more.

Without warning, the stagecoach shuddered to a stop. The unexpected movement jerked them back against the seat. Seconds later, the door swung open and sounds of exited chatter from a group of waiting passengers filled the small interior compartment.

"End of the line, folks," the round-faced driver called out, his deep voice at odds with the boyish face.

Tim muttered something under his breath and released her.

The driver held out his hand to Cassidy but his apologetic smile was directed at both of them. "Sorry about the bump earlier. Have to admit I didn't see the rut until I'd hit it. Anyway, I hope you folks enjoyed the ride."

"Loved it." Cassidy flashed the man a brilliant smile then glanced back at Tim. "I wish it had lasted a little longer, though. I wasn't quite ready for it to end."

Street dances had never appealed to Caro. Tim had thought his wife's objections made a lot of sense: intoxicated people who didn't know the first thing about how to properly dance making fools of themselves. Consequently, during their marriage, they'd never once come down to West Deloney during Old West Days.

Yet, here Tim stood on this last weekend in May gyrating with Cassidy and hundreds of strangers. The scene in this section of downtown Jackson bore a distinct resemblance to Times Square on New Year's Eve. Music blasted from a popular regional band who'd taken the stage in front of the local theater. There was vitality and electricity in the air that Tim found contagious.

He couldn't believe the number of people he knew—and the number Cassidy knew—who stopped to bump and grind beside them before moving on. After a particularly fine rock classic that got everyone's blood pumping, Tim concluded he'd definitely been missing something all these years.

Granted, this was a far different atmosphere than a dance at the Spring Gulch Country Club with fine cuisine and music from a band attired in black tie. This was loud and dusty and a bit uncivilized. Enjoyable, but in an entirely different way.

The rock song ended and the band immediately launched into a sultry rhythm that quickly became a pulsating beat in his blood. Cassidy's hands encircled his neck and her hips began to sway in a sexy samba.

Their eyes locked and Tim found himself drowning in the liquid blue depths. The people surrounding them faded into nothingness and all he saw was her.

Tim barely noticed the music had ended, scarcely heard the lead singer announce the band was taking a break. His hands were on Cassidy's waist and his eyes trained on that sexy mouth.

God, he wanted her.

"Break it up, you two. This is a family event."

Tim groaned and dropped his hands from Cassidy's waist.

Liam Gallagher, old friend and the reason that Tim was on this date in the first place, slapped Tim on the back. "Haven't seen you in weeks and where do I run into you? At a street dance of all places. Unbelievable."

"Cassidy. Good to see you." Liam's smile widened. He jerked a thumb in Tim's direction. "I haven't had a chance to thank you for bidding on this guy."

"My good deed of the month," she said with a cheeky smile, not appearing off balance by Liam's unexpected appearance. Then again, Cassidy always seemed to handle whatever life tossed her way with a smile and an impudent attitude.

The two bantered like old friends about the auction, or as Liam dubbed it, the "Jackson Hole Meat Market."

Tim watched the two, an uneasy knot forming in his gut. Women liked Liam. He was a good-looking guy with thick brown hair, and his smile always seemed to make the ladies swoon. Not to mention the psychologist could converse easily with anyone. Over the years Tim had developed that skill but the art of small talk still didn't come naturally.

Liam paused, as if suddenly realizing only he and Cassidy were engaged in conversation. "Am I interrupting?"

Tim met his friend's gaze. "Ever heard the saying 'three is a crowd'?"

Liam laughed uproariously as if Tim had made a joke. But within minutes, the psychologist had come up with an excuse to leave.

Tim thought he'd once again have Cassidy to himself but Liam had barely disappeared when he caught sight of Jayne Connors headed in their direction.

Though known for her tailored dresses and heels, apparently in concession to the casualness of the event, tonight Jayne wore navy pants and a sleeveless white shirt.

When her gaze landed on Tim, she waved and smiled.

Her bright smile dimmed when she caught sight of Cassidy. The look of disbelief she shot him made no sense. Tim distinctly remembered mentioning his date with Cassidy to her.

"What a surprise." Tim offered a welcoming smile when she drew close. "I thought you didn't care for these kinds of events."

"Back at you."

Tim sensed Cassidy's watchful gaze on him.

"I was wrong," he told Jayne. "It's fun."

Cassidy offered the woman a friendly smile. "Good to see you, Jayne."

"You, too, Cassidy."

To Tim's surprise there seemed to be genuine warmth between the women. He hadn't realized they were so well acquainted.

"The Jackson Chamber of Commerce has been plugging Old West Days all week," Jayne explained. "Since I didn't have plans for the evening I decided I'd wander around and see what the hype was all about."

Cassidy lifted a hand as if in mock toast, approval in her eyes. "I salute your spirit of adventure."

Though she looked pleased, Jayne lifted one shoulder. "It's not as enjoyable when you're by yourself."

"Join us." Tim spoke without thinking.

"Yes, please join us," Cassidy echoed, though with less than her normal exuberance.

"That's kind of you both to offer, but you caught me on my way back to the car." Jayne pressed two fingers against her temple. "The music, the heat, the noise is giving me a headache."

Tim was struck by the words. Only moments before Cassidy had confessed to Liam that the crowds and the noise energized her. Still, he could understand how Jayne might find the whole scene overwhelming. If he'd ever been able to drag Caro here, she'd likely have headed home with a headache, too.

"Feel better." Cassidy touched Jayne's arm. "I'll see you Monday. If you need to reschedule—"

"I'm fine," Jayne assured her. "I'll definitely be there."

Tim tilted his head.

"Haircut," Jayne informed him. "Nobody cuts hair like Cassidy."

"You're too kind." Cassidy's quicksilver grin flashed. "Though it's completely true."

The band launched their next set with a Southern rock favorite from the sixties. The popular tune was apparently familiar to many in the crowd and en masse they began to sing the words.

The librarian winced. "That's my exit cue."

With a pained look on her face, Jayne said her good-byes and hurried off.

When Cassidy tugged on his arm, Tim leaned close, inhaling a whiff of her perfume. Something about the enticing scent made him want to move closer.

"Let's explore." As she spoke her hand slid down his arm and her fingers laced with his.

Her hand wrapped in his felt so natural, Tim didn't even think of pulling away. Deliberately heading in a direction away from the band, they wove through the crowd. It took several blocks before the streets and sidewalks became less crowded. Instead of loud and pulsating, the music became festive background noise.

With no destination in mind, he and Cassidy wandered, strolling side by side, enjoying the warm summer breeze and each other's company.

After several blocks the streets grew crowded once again and Tim quickly discovered the reason. Vendors. Booths stood like soldiers at attention, lining both sides of the street. Tim's gaze swept over signs touting everything from cotton candy to rings made from horseshoe nails. Cassidy paused at one of the first booths, where an older gentleman dressed as an Old West sheriff stood selling tin stars.

"Give me your opinion." Tim slanted a questioning look in Cassidy's direction. "Think the girls would get a kick out of one?"

For a moment Cassidy silently stared at the badges, her expression unreadable.

"I wanted one in the worst way when I was their age," she said finally, almost to herself.

"Really?"

She nodded. "I had this crazy idea the badge would give me superpowers and allow me to control those around me. Stupid."

Something in the way she spoke, or maybe it was the turbulent emotion in her eyes, had him reaching for her hand and giving it a squeeze. "Did you ever get one?"

A shadow passed over her face. "Naw. But that was okay. It wouldn't have helped anyway."

Glancing away, she focused on a teenage girl walking by with a cone of rainbow-colored cotton candy. She touched his arm. "Be right back."

She did that a lot, he realized, little squeezes and pats. His family wasn't overly demonstrative but he liked it when Cassidy touched him. And the contact made him want to touch her back.

The line for the tin stars moved quickly. After making his purchase, Tim started down the sidewalk toward the cotton-candy seller. He thought back, trying to recall what he knew of Cassidy's childhood. She'd been several years behind him in school. There had been a lot of talk when the pigtailed blonde from the wrong side of the tracks had worn a Halloween cat costume to school most of her kindergarten year.

But the incident Tim recalled most vividly was the time Cassidy had shaved her head. She'd been in fifth or sixth grade at the time. The buzz she'd created when she came to school demanding everyone call her Sinéad had lingered for weeks.

As far as Tim knew no one ever figured out what that was all about. Some blamed the incident on her crazy mother, who wasn't exactly a stellar influence. Others said it was a need to stand out, brought on by an absentee father.

"Tim."

He blinked and saw Cassidy approaching him, holding two cones of rainbow cotton candy. "I got one for each of us."

He took the spun sugar, deciding it wouldn't hurt to ignore proper nutrition for one evening. "I have something for you, too."

Reaching into his pocket, Tim pulled out a tin star and pressed it into her hand.

She stared at it then up at him, her expression questioning.

"Better late than never," he quipped when she remained silent. "Perhaps you'll finally get those superpowers."

Her fingers curled around the star and she slipped it into her purse. She cleared her throat before speaking. "Thanks."

"Thank you for the cotton candy." He took a bite and had to admit the fluff tasted as good as he remembered. Plucking off another piece, he held it between his thumb and forefinger for a second before popping it into his mouth. "What's next on the agenda?"

"Do you like rodeos?" She gazed up at him, a hopeful gleam in her eyes, a faint smear of sugar on her full lips.

Tim forced his gaze from the lips that reminded him of delicious pink strawberries.

Rodeos, he reminded himself. They were talking about

bulls, broncs and roping. Despite growing up in Wyoming, Tim had little exposure to the sport. His parents had never taken him or his sisters to the rodeo. Caro had never expressed an interest and he hadn't cared enough to press the issue.

Tim saw the look in Cassidy's eyes. She wanted to go and he'd made it clear from the start he would go along with whatever she wanted.

Besides, so far he'd enjoyed everything about the evening she'd orchestrated, including riding the bull at Wally's place. "Sounds like fun."

She flashed a bright smile and took his arm.

An easy breeze ruffled her hair but Cassidy made no move to push it back into place. He liked that about her, too. Unlike those women who needed to be perfectly groomed at all times, Cassidy gave herself permission to revel in the moment.

Tonight, he'd gone with the flow and as a result felt more like the kid he'd once been than a widowed father of two with heavy responsibilities. As they started down the street in the direction of his car, his gaze kept returning to her mouth.

All too soon the evening would draw to a close. Though it had been a long time since he'd dated, from everything he'd heard and read, a good-night kiss was practically expected in today's dating world.

Although this wasn't really a date, not in the true sense of the word, he was determined to savor every moment and fulfill all her expectations. If that meant a good-night kiss, so be it.

He only hoped he could stop at one.

## Chapter Four

After spending several hours at the rodeo, watching everything from father-and-son team roping to kids chasing ties on calves, Cassidy noticed Tim stifling a yawn when he thought she wasn't looking. Reluctantly, Cassidy decided it was time to call it a night.

Still, she dragged her feet as Tim walked her up the flight of steps to the apartment over her salon in downtown Jackson. Hands down, the evening had qualified as the best of her life.

"Want to come inside for a few minutes?" Cassidy unlocked the door and opened it wide, keeping her tone casual.

Tim hesitated.

Cassidy held her breath.

"Sure," he said after an endless moment. "I'd love to come in."

She dropped her bag to the sofa and, out of the corner of her eye, saw him survey the tiny apartment. She knew where he lived, a big house in the Spring Gulch subdivision, just outside of Jackson. Though she'd never been inside his home, she'd attended many parties in the area and knew the opulence of the residences.

What did he see when he looked around the small two-bedroom unit she called home? The tiny rooms? The lack of amenities? When his gaze lingered on the overstuffed sofa, she wondered if he recognized it as coming from the big-box store on the edge of town.

At least he would find no fault with her housekeeping. After growing up in squalor, in dirty rooms so crowded with junk you could scarcely see the floor, Cassidy was frightfully neat. Though most of the money she made went straight back into her business, it had been important to Cassidy to create a home, not simply just have a place to sleep.

To brighten the room she'd added a variety of pillows to the sofa. Paintings, done by local artists, hung on the walls, adding additional color.

Tim rocked back on his heels. "Your place has a nice feel."

Pleasure rippled through her at the obvious approval in his voice.

"Thank you." Cassidy kept her tone nonchalant. "Can I get you something to drink? I have beer, wine, soda or water."

"Water sounds good."

In the kitchen Cassidy retrieved two tumblers from cabinets painted a cheery sunshine yellow and quickly filled them with ice and water. She returned to the living room and placed the glasses on a flat steamer trunk that doubled as a much-needed storage spot and served as a coffee table.

When Tim took a seat on the sofa, she sat beside him, though not as close as she'd have liked. Something warned her if she moved too fast, she might spook him.

Or…perhaps not. When she gazed into his eyes, there was heat smoldering, which she hadn't expected. Still, Cassidy kept the conversation deliberately light as they talked about the high points of the evening, then about her salon and his medical practice before moving on to his daughters.

Hearing the pride in his voice, seeing the love in his eyes when he spoke of "the girls," made Cassidy's heart ache just a little. She had no idea who her own father was, or even if the man was still alive.

Over the years there'd been a succession of men in and out of the shack where she lived with her mother. When Cassidy had once quipped they should put in a revolving door, she'd gotten a backhand across the mouth and a bloody lip.

Not wanting to go down the same path as her mother, Cassidy had been careful in her own life. Some of the men she'd dated had the mistaken impression she was easy. That was far from the truth. Cassidy had only been with two men, both of whom she cared for and she'd been convinced they cared for her. They'd cared, but they hadn't loved her.

She needed to be loved. Totally. Completely. And she refused to settle for less.

Nearly another hour passed before Tim stretched. "I suppose I should be heading home."

Her heart flip-flopped but, despite his words, he remained seated.

"What's the hurry?" She kept her tone light, her smile easy.

"It's been a long day," he said, then settled back and told her about twin babies he'd delivered before dawn.

"You should have said something." At the rodeo she'd observed him yawning. Now, for the first time, she noticed the lines of fatigue edging his eyes. "We could have rescheduled."

"Never crossed my mind." His lips tipped upward. "I enjoyed every bit of the evening."

"Even when the drunk cowboy stomped on your foot at the street dance?"

Tim winced. "Not that, but everything else."

"I had a fab time, too." She leaned forward, brushed her lips lightly against his. "Thank you for a wonderful evening and the tin star."

She waited for him to say they'd have to do it again. Instead he cupped her face in his hands and gazed at her. In seconds the eye contact turned into something more, a tangible connection between the two of them. "You're a wonderful woman, Cassidy Kaye."

Then he did what she'd been hoping he'd do since he arrived at her door. He kissed her, long and slow and deep.

He tasted like the most decadent candy, and like a child who had never been given enough, she wanted more. Lots more.

So Cassidy did the only thing a woman faced with such a situation could do—she wrapped her arms around his neck and took another helping.

"I'll definitely consider your offer." Jewel Lucas leaned forward on the small table at the Hill of Beans coffee shop, her entire attention focused on Cassidy.

"I'm a joy to work with," Cassidy told her. "Just ask me."

"Modest, too." Jewel laughed. The sunshine through the window caught the wisp of red in her auburn hair. She was a pretty woman with thick curls tumbling to her shoulders and emerald-colored eyes. In her jeans and striped summer tee, she could more easily pass for a college girl than a mother of a boy ready for middle school.

Until this morning, Cassidy's interaction with Jewel had been confined to a smile and a brief hello if they passed each other on the street. Today, they'd bonded over chocolate-chip bagels with cream cheese and lattes made with whole milk.

Playing detective, Cassidy discovered that prior to coming to Jackson Hole to live with her grandparents, Jewel's life had been one of turmoil. The fact that they both had mothers who cared more for their drugs and boyfriends than their daughters had been an instant bond between the two women.

When Cassidy asked Jewel if she'd like to earn extra money doing makeup for weddings and other events, Jewel had seemed genuinely intrigued. Best of all, she hadn't said no. Not yet, anyway.

A car backfired on the street, drawing Cassidy's gaze out the window. Her heart hitched. But as the guy drew closer, Cassidy saw the tall, broad-shouldered man wasn't Tim. Other than being about the same height and build, the two didn't even resemble each other.

"Earth to Cassidy."

Cassidy turned back to find Jewel staring at her with a bemused smile over the rim of her cappuccino cup.

"You promised to tell me about Old West Days. But—" Jewel glanced at her phone and made a face at the time displayed "—you have to get back to the salon and I have to get home to the ranch. So just give me the good stuff."

"Good stuff?"

"You're stalling." Jewel pointed a finger at her. "I'm talking hot cowboys with big, ah, Stetsons."

Cassidy realized during the entire course of the evening she hadn't seen a single hot cowboy. That was a first. "There weren't any."

She heard the note of stunned disbelief in her voice.

"They were there." Jewel rolled her eyes. "You just weren't looking. You had eyes only for the handsome doctor."

Probably true, but this type of speculation was something Cassidy needed to nip in the bud. She carelessly waved a hand in the air. "It was an arranged thing. I guess I felt I owed Tim my full attention."

Her tone was offhand, just as she intended. It would never do for word to get around that she was hung up on Dr. Tim Duggan. Especially with the attraction being one-sided.

"Did he ask you out again?"

The hopeful gleam in Jewel's eyes surprised her. She wouldn't have guessed the woman was a romantic. Cassidy decided not to hold this fact against Jewel.

"Of course not. We didn't go on a real date. It was just a bachelor-auction payment thing."

Jewel's brows pulled together. "You had a good time and enjoyed each other's company, right?"

"A second date wasn't part of the deal." An unexpected lump rose to Cassidy's throat. She cleared it before continuing. "I don't expect to hear from him again."

"It's only Monday." Jewel made it sound as if a couple days of silence after a fabulous evening were no big deal. "He's probably one of those guys who follow the three-day rule."

As far as Cassidy was concerned, waiting three days to call someone you were interested in seeing again—just so you wouldn't appear too eager—was incredibly juvenile. When Cassidy found herself hoping that was the reason, rather than the fact that Tim simply didn't care, she realized Jewel wasn't the only one with a romantic heart.

"I have to get back to work." Suddenly edgy and more than a little irritated with herself because it did matter, Cassidy pushed back her chair and stood.

Jewel rose and they left the coffee shop together, splitting off in different directions once they reached the sidewalk.

Lost in thought, Cassidy flipped into autopilot mode and turned toward her salon.

The truth was, things couldn't have gone better on the date. Tim had lightened up considerably under her teasing. They'd ridden the mechanical bull, eaten cotton candy and danced. He'd bought her a gift.

*A tin star.*

Exactly like the one she'd wanted so desperately as a child. The badge was now tucked safely into one of the pockets of her large zebra-striped bag. As she pushed open the door to the salon, Cassidy resisted the urge to take the badge out and gaze at it one more time.

"Look what came for you," Daffodil Prentiss, one of the stylists, announced before the salon door even had a chance to close.

Cassidy came to an abrupt halt. She widened her eyes to take in the huge bouquet of Gerbera daisies taking up most of the reception desk counter. The bright, flashy colors drew her to the flowers like a moth to a flame. Her heart skipped a beat. "These are mine?"

"Your name is on the card." With well-practiced ease, Daffy put a customer under the dryer then stepped forward.

"They're quite lovely, don't you think?" Kathy Randall, Cassidy's next appointment, piped up from her seat in the waiting area. Ignoring the magazine lying open in her lap, she stared at Cassidy and the bouquet with undisguised interest.

Cassidy had no doubt word that she'd received flowers would be all over Jackson by nightfall. Kathy was extremely well connected in the community. Her son, Tripp, was the mayor of Jackson.

Reverently, Cassidy touched the edge of a hot-pink petal with the tip of one finger. No one had ever given her flowers before, not even a basket on May Day when she'd been a kid. Of course, in her neighborhood, any bas-

ket left would likely have been stolen off the porch before
the recipient opened the door.

She couldn't imagine who would have sent them. A satisfied customer? Perhaps a bride, thanking her for making
her special day even more special?

"Here." Daffy reached into the bouquet then pressed
the card she'd retrieved into Cassidy's hand. "You should
read—"

The waiflike blonde with the huge blue eyes and gentle
spirit appeared to reconsider what she'd been about to say.

"Or do it later." Daffy spoke quickly, her cheeks now a
deep pink. "Your two o'clock is here."

"I don't mind waiting," Kathy Randall protested.

Deliberately slipping the card into her pocket, Cassidy
smiled at Kathy and spoke loudly enough for everyone.
"Tell me that today is the day you're going to let me add
a pretty pink streak to your hair."

The entire salon erupted in laughter at the thought of
the mayor's proper mother going pink.

Crisis averted.

While the flowers *could* be from a bride or a customer,
the bouquet was too perfectly chosen to have come from
anyone but Tim.


Cassidy didn't have to worry about seeing Tim at the
book club meeting at Mary Karen and Travis Fisher's home
the following night. While many of the women brought
their husbands or boyfriends for a meal prior to the book
discussion, Tim had no reason to be in attendance.

Jayne also wasn't part of the book club group. For Cassidy, tonight marked only her second meeting.

When Hailey Ferris, speech therapist by day, makeup
artist extraordinaire by night, had approached Cassidy several months earlier about joining the group, Cassidy had
been hesitant. Granted, most of the women in the group

were friends. They were also doctors and lawyers or wives of doctors and lawyers.

*Snooty society women.* Her mother's slurred words echoed in her head. *Think they're better than us.*

But Cassidy had reminded herself that second-class was merely a state of mind. And she refused to think of herself as less than anyone else.

She'd accepted the invitation.

Last month's book had been difficult to get through and not at all enjoyable. But the book Mary Karen Fisher had chosen for this evening, *Naked in Death*, by J.D. Robb, had been devoured in one evening.

Cassidy identified with the spunky Eve Dallas, who'd had a horrible childhood but had made something of herself. She liked it that Roarke, Eve's love interest, could see beneath the detective's brash exterior.

She only wished Tim had been equally mesmerized by her. But as she parked her car and walked to the front porch of Mary Karen's large two-story home in the mountains surrounding Jackson, Cassidy told herself that a relationship between her and the dedicated doctor apparently wasn't meant to be.

That was why he'd sent the flowers, thanking her for a lovely evening and wishing her only the best in the future. It had been a brush-off, a classy one but a brush-off just the same.

While initially disappointed—the empty pint of Ben & Jerry's Phish Food in the garbage was proof of that—Cassidy certainly didn't want any man who didn't want her. She had a lot to offer. If Tim Duggan was too nearsighted to see she was a gem, well, it was his loss.

Cassidy lifted her hand to knock only to have the door flung open before her knuckles reached the wood.

"Mo-om," a boy about ten with thick curly blond hair

and bright blue eyes bellowed in a surprisingly strong voice. "Another lady is here. This one has pink hair."

Actually, it was only the tips that were edged in pink. Cassidy recognized the child as one of Mary Karen's oldest set of twins. Since the boys were identical, she wasn't sure if he was Connor or Caleb.

Mary Karen rushed into the foyer. The mother of five was a pretty, petite woman with a mass of blond curls and big blue eyes. Her husband, Travis, was a successful OB in practice with Tim. "Connor, there's no need to yell."

"I didn't yell." His jaw jutted out. "I—"

"You know, I believe I saw Finley taking a fresh batch of mozzarella sticks downstairs," Mary Karen said, interrupting her son.

Connor's eyes filled with alarm. "Not fair. Caleb will eat them all."

The boy sprinted off, leaving the two women alone.

"I'm so happy you made it." Mary Karen held out her hands to Cassidy, pulling her in for a brief hug.

"I loved the book," Cassidy told her hostess as the two crossed the spacious foyer with the gleaming hardwood floors.

"It sure beats *She's Come Undone*." The pretty blonde made a face and they both laughed. "That one had me depressed for weeks."

The Wally Lamb bestseller had been the previous month's selection and Cassidy agreed with MK's assessment. If it hadn't been for the camaraderie among the women, Cassidy might not have returned.

That would have been a shame because this was a great group of women and Cassidy enjoyed them. The actual book discussion wasn't even a large part of the evening. Mostly they drank wine, ate gourmet food and caught up on each other's busy lives.

Mary Karen slipped an arm through Cassidy's, leaned

close and spoke in a conspiratorial whisper. "Just FYI, Lexi and Nick are in Texas this month so I made the entrée. If it tastes hideous, pretend to like it so everyone will agree it's fabulous. Sort of an Emperor's-new-clothes kind of thing."

Cassidy nodded but wasn't sure why Mary Karen worried. Food was food, right? While Lexi's gourmet entrées were always the talk of the book club, Cassidy was easily pleased. She'd be satisfied with ramen noodles and beer.

They reached the great room just as loud cheers of the masculine variety came from outside. Cassidy slanted a questioning glance in Mary Karen's direction.

"The boys—oh, I'm sorry—the *men* are playing basketball." The hostess gave an indulgent laugh. "Though we all know they act more like little boys when they get together."

"Mrs. Fisher." Finley Davis, the teenage daughter of Dr. Michelle Davis, a local OB, came up from the stairs leading down into the basement. "Is it okay if Mickey and I start a movie for some of the smaller kids?"

"Absolutely." Mary Karen gave the girl, apparently one of several babysitters for the evening, an approving smile. "Let me show you where we keep the remote."

As Cassidy watched MK hurry off, she recalled the "rules." Whoever hosted the book club hired babysitters to watch the children of the attendees. Cassidy was one of the few single persons in the group. Her thoughts slipped briefly to Tim.

What would it be like to share an evening like this—one surrounded by mutual friends—with him?

"Cassidy. What are you doing here?"

For a second she thought she'd conjured up Tim's image. She blinked once. Blinked again. Huh, still there.

Despite the "have a happy life" bouquet of flowers brush-off, she was genuinely pleased to see him. Even with sweat beading his brow and that lean, muscular body clad in gray gym shorts and a faded green T-shirt, he looked amazing.

He stared at her expectantly and she realized he'd asked a question. Frazzled, she tried to recall what it was. Oh, yes, something about not expecting to see her here. "I came for the book club. What about you?"

"Basketball." He wiped the perspiration from his forehead with the back of his hand. "And it gives the girls a chance to play with some of their friends."

"Esther and Ellyn are here?"

"Downstairs." He smiled, the way he always did when mentioning his daughters. "We'll stay for dinner then head out."

"Thanks again for the flowers." Cassidy decided she might as well get the niceties out of the way. She'd called last night to thank him personally, but had been forced to leave a message when she'd reached his voice mail. "They were beautiful."

"I had a great time." He rocked back on his sneakers, looking suddenly uncomfortable. "I'd have suggested we see each other again but—"

"Hey, it was a one-night thing." Cassidy waved a hand. "It—"

"One-night thing." Dr. Travis Fisher appeared out of nowhere, as if conjured up by a magician's wand.

A tall, lanky man with sandy-colored hair, Travis always held a mischievous gleam in his eyes. Despite being a father of five and a respected doctor in the largest OB practice in the region, Travis had a playful, approachable side that Cassidy found refreshing in someone so prominent.

Travis crossed his arms, looking decidedly un-doctor-like in his sweaty gym clothes. His gaze slid expectantly from Tim to her. "Details are necessary for absolution. Confess to Father Travis, my children."

Cassidy rolled her eyes. "Sorry to disappoint, Father

Travis. Tim and I simply attended Old West Days together. A bachelor-auction date, hence the one-night-thing."

"I heard you'd purchased my partner." Travis's lips turned down in mock sorrow as he glanced from her to Tim and back again. "Perhaps next year, you'll do better with your money."

The man was so doggone charming Cassidy had to chuckle. "Perhaps."

"Hey," Tim protested. "We had fun."

"We did." Cassidy kept her tone light and breezy then glanced toward the kitchen. "I better see if MK needs help."

Travis took a step, effectively blocking the escape route. "Have you heard the saying 'Too many cooks spoil the soup'?"

"No," Cassidy said honestly.

Travis chuckled. "It means you have something more important to do than assist my lovely wife."

Cassidy shot him a suspicious glance. "And what exactly would that be?"

"I want to hear more about your night with my associate. He's been disappointingly closemouthed." Travis glanced at his colleague and shook his head, actually clucking his tongue.

Tim's jaw jutted out in a stubborn tilt. "Personal activities are not appropriate topics of conversation in a medical setting."

*That could be the reason*, Cassidy thought. Or perhaps he simply didn't want to advertise the fact he'd been with her.

The thought was a punch to the heart.

"We're not at the clinic or the hospital now," Travis pointed out. He turned to Cassidy. "I hear you got on the bull."

"Have you ever tried it?" Cassidy asked, attempting to steer the conversation toward Travis.

But the doctor was a master of redirection and before he walked away, Travis had managed to ferret out every detail of her Saturday night activities. Everything except the kissing she and Tim had done on the sofa.

"The man is a barracuda," Cassidy murmured as, apparently satisfied, Travis strolled off whistling.

"You have to remember, he raised seven younger siblings. Now he has five kids of his own." Tim's lips quirked up. "He knows how to get answers fast."

"I bared my soul," Cassidy said, still in a state of stunned disbelief.

"Not quite." Though there was no one within earshot, Tim lowered his voice. "You made him believe I walked you to the door and left."

The look in his eyes sent heat spurting through her veins. Until she reminded herself that all he wanted from her was friendship.

"I didn't think you'd want it broadcasted around Jackson Hole that you'd been making out with a hairstylist." Cassidy gave a mock shudder. "Not good for your street cred."

His hand closed around her arm. "Is that what you really think? That I'm ashamed of you?"

The anger in his voice surprised her.

"It doesn't matter." She met his gaze. "Saturday night is the past. And you and I are back to what we were before."

"What exactly is that?"

She looped her arm through his and offered a cheeky grin. "Why, friends, of course."

## Chapter Five

She wanted to be his *friend*.

Tim didn't know whether to be relieved or disappointed. As he ate, he watched Cassidy out of the corner of his eye. She looked exceeding pretty in a shiny hot-pink shirt that matched the tips of color in her hair. The silver pants that hugged her long legs added a sexy vibe.

It wasn't simply her attractiveness that drew people to her. Cassidy Kaye radiated life and had a joyous energy that was incredibly appealing.

More often than not when he glanced in her direction, she was laughing or making someone else smile. Though Tim heard someone say this was only her second time coming to the book club, he'd never have known it.

She fit right in with these successful, intelligent women. He could easily see why they'd wanted her to be part of their group.

All too soon the meal was over. The dishes were cleared. The women immediately staked their claim on

the large oval table in the country kitchen. The husbands—
and boyfriends—swarmed into the great room, where the
large flat screen was tuned to a popular sports channel.

After dinner, Tim had planned to get the twins and head
home. But his friends encouraged him to hang out longer.
When he checked on his daughters and discovered them
having fun, he decided to stay.

Almost two hours later he found himself walking out
with the crowd.

"Your hair is pretty," he heard Esther say.

Of his two girls, Esther was the one who talked the
most, while her shy sister usually held back.

He turned to see who his daughter was speaking with
and discovered it was Cassidy.

"Thank you." Cassidy sounded pleased. "I like yours,
too."

Her fingers, the nails a vivid blue, flicked one of his
daughter's braids. "Did your dad do these for you?"

Esther dissolved in laughter. "Daddy can't braid hair."

"Grandma did it," Ellyn said so softly Tim wondered
if Cassidy heard. From the smile the hairstylist bestowed
on his youngest—by two minutes—he figured she had.

"Stellar job." Cassidy gazed thoughtfully at the braids.
"It'd be extra pretty if you wove a ribbon through the
braid."

Esther's eyes widened. "Can you do that?"

"It's easy," Cassidy said. "I do it all the time."

"Your hair is pink," Ellyn murmured as they continued
down the walk to the edge of the road, where most of the
cars were parked.

"Ellyn," Tim said sharply.

Cassidy shot him a surprised look. "It's okay. The tips
are actually fuchsia."

She pulled her attention back to the girls. "Since hair

is my business, I change my color whenever I want. It's kind of expected."

"Could you make my hair purple?" Esther's voice trembled with eagerness. "It's my favorite color."

An image of his mother's face flashed before Tim. He had no doubt she'd burst into flames if either of her granddaughters appeared on her doorstep with purple hair.

Cassidy slanted a sideways glance at Tim. "I can do practically anything with hair. Now, tell me what kind of games you were playing downstairs. It sounded like so much fun, I thought about leaving the book club to join you."

Tim had also been curious about the shrieks of laughter coming from the basement. From what his daughters described, it sounded like a Wii bowling-gone-wild session followed by an old-fashioned game of Twister.

Before he could ask any questions or even have a chance to visit with Cassidy, they were at his SUV.

Cassidy smiled brightly at the three of them.

"Safe trip home." With a jaunty wave of her hand, she sauntered off.

Tim couldn't help noticing how her hips swayed enticingly from side to side in those sexy silver pants.

"She's pretty," Esther declared, touching one of her braids.

"I like her," Ellyn added, her little face serious.

"I like her, too," Tim said then unlocked the car doors so they could begin their way down the mountain toward home.

Cassidy kept busy the rest of the week. Not working Saturday had caused her to schedule clients late every evening, except for the night she'd attended book club.

She'd enjoyed the discussion and the chance to relax. It struck her that most of her interactions with the other women had, up to this point, mostly been confined to work activities.

Oh, there had been the occasional parties tossed into the mix, but simply socializing with other women in a group had been outside her wheelhouse.

The book club had been pleasant and they hadn't run out of things to discuss. Since the group included several doctors as well as physical and speech therapists, there had been a lot of medical talk...which she found fascinating. They'd seemed equally interested in her efforts to expand her business and garner some of the fun—and lucrative—wedding trade.

Now Saturday had rolled around again. She'd spent the entire day out of the salon. This time because of a wedding. Thankfully, it had turned out to be a beautiful June day with a cloudless blue sky and only the barest hint of a breeze. With temperatures in the low seventies, the day could not have been more perfect for an outdoor afternoon ceremony.

She'd arrived early for bridal-party hair and makeup. Moments before, she'd just retouched the hair of the wedding party while endless post-ceremony pictures were taken.

Dinner was next on the agenda, to be served in elegant style in one of the large white tents erected on the ranch property, followed by a dance with an open bar.

Cassidy had been invited to stay for the wedding and participate in the festivities, but she planned to leave now that the last of the pictures had been taken. The bride and her attendants would be on their own.

She packed up her bag of beauty supplies and slung it over her shoulder, then turned toward her car. Cassidy was so focused on skirting several groups of people it took her a moment to realize someone was calling her name.

Then a hand closed around her arm and she smelled

him, that faint intoxicating scent of bergamot and sandal-
wood.

With her heart doing a salsa against her ribs, she lifted
her head and gazed into Tim's hazel eyes.

"You're headed the wrong way." Tim nearly groaned
aloud at the comment. *Smooth, Duggan, really smooth.*

He told himself he'd been startled, surprised to see the
pretty blonde making her way against the crowd toward
the field where the cars were parked.

Tim had never considered he'd run into Cassidy at his
cousin Veronica's wedding. Not that he knew his cousin
or her fiancé all that well. They were second or third re-
lations once removed or something like that, but family
was family.

"Tim." She glanced around. "I didn't think you'd be
here."

"I just arrived. My parents and the girls are around
somewhere." He took her arm and tugged her from the
stream of humanity. "We planned to go to the ceremony
together but a baby decided this afternoon was her time to
be born. I told them I'd try to meet them at the reception."

"Great suit."

Tim glanced down. Dark charcoal pinstriped suit, white
shirt and red paisley tie. Nothing special. Unlike Cassidy,
who looked stunning.

His gaze slid over her slender form, clad in a sexy black
dress with a revealing deep V and red heels. "You're looking pretty spiffy yourself tonight."

*Spiffy.* He stifled a groan. A sixteen-year-old could do
better.

"I meant *lovely*," he said. "You look very lovely."

She gave him a wink. "I prefer *spiffy*."

"Well, Miss Spiffy, I hate to tell you but you're going
the wrong way."

"My duty is done." At his apparently blank look, she

continued, "Veronica's and her attendants' hair is now in their own hands."

He frowned. "She didn't invite you to stay for the reception?"

"She invited," Cassidy quickly assured him. "But I'm considering other options."

"By how you're dressed, it looks as if you planned to stay."

She lifted a shoulder in a slight shrug. "It's been a long week. I'm not in the mood for socializing with a bunch of strangers."

That wasn't the entire truth. Cassidy had gotten a call from her mother, Crystal, that morning that had left her out of sorts. A call from an unexpected place: St. Louis, Missouri. Even worse, Crystal had asked for bail money, for her and her current "fiancé."

It was drug charges—again—specifically possession with intent to distribute. According to her mother, the heroin had been planted. When Cassidy made it clear she wouldn't be sending any money, the raging had started. Cassidy had hung up, but her normally sunny mood had turned overcast.

"I'm not really in the mood for socializing, either," he told her.

Her lips turned up. "Well, then, I think you've come to the wrong place."

Tim's gaze slid across her face. The smile didn't reach her eyes. She looked troubled, he realized. No, not troubled, sad. He couldn't remember ever seeing her anything but bright and chipper. But then, he didn't really know her that well.

"Come with me," he said impulsively. "We'll grab some dinner."

She shook her head, not interested in facing his mother and her disapproving looks. Most days, Cassidy found

Suzanne Duggan's dislike of her rather humorous. This wasn't one of those days. Today she felt raw and vulnerable. "I planned to catch something quick then go for a run."

"You run?"

His look of shock made her smile. She trailed her fingers down the side of her dress. "How do you think I keep this splendiferous figure?"

"And a fine figure it is." Tim started to say more then realized that would be inappropriate. "Want company?"

Surprise widened Cassidy's vivid blue eyes. "What about your parents and daughters?"

"I told them I wasn't sure I'd be able to make it tonight." Tim stuffed his hands into his pockets. "My mother will be in her element, parading the girls around like trick ponies. I'd only be in the way."

Knowing his mother, Cassidy was skeptical. This was a family affair. Suzanne would want her son, the prominent doctor, at her side.

Cassidy had a good idea what was going on here. He didn't want to stay and was using her as an excuse. Still, she couldn't bring herself to blow him off. "You're hardly dressed for a run."

"Back at you."

The ridiculous retort made her laugh.

"C'mon, Cass." His tone turned persuasive. "It's been a really long day. The girls are safe and happy with my parents. I could use a break."

It had been a long day for her, too. While Veronica was a nice enough woman, she'd been a demanding bride. Her attendants were cut from the same mold. When Cassidy added her mother's call to the equation, a run was a necessity.

If Tim wanted to come along, well, she wouldn't stop him. "Will you be able to keep up?"

He smiled. "Watch me."

\* \* \*

By the time they reached their vehicles, Cassidy had come up with a plan. Tim would stop home and change, then pick her up at her place. While the sun was still high in the sky, they'd drive to Goodwin Lake Trail. The popular trail started at eight thousand feet elevation and ended at a lovely lake. Using the lake as a turnaround point would give her and Tim a five-mile run.

As Cassidy pulled on her black running shorts, sports bra and purple tank, she wondered if this impulsive move was a mistake. She immediately dismissed the worry. They were friends and, after the distress of hearing from her mother, it would be nice to have someone to distract her.

It wasn't as if Tim was an annoying chatterbox. They'd probably run and not exchange five words. But he would be there beside her.

Cassidy quickly realized she'd been wrong. From the time Tim picked her up, the popular doctor kept the conversation going.

As he relayed anecdotes about his girls and his parents, Cassidy began to relax. She and Tim were pretty equal in their running fitness and they settled easily into a comfortable rhythm on the gradual climb to the lake.

"How'd you hook up with my cousin?" Tim asked as the pristine Alpine lake came into view.

"Who?"

"Veronica."

"Oh." Cassidy realized she'd already put the bride into her "thank God that one is done" mental file cabinet. "I did the hair of one of her friends last year. She approached me."

"You have my sympathy."

Cassidy was enough of a businesswoman to at least pretend not to understand.

"I was never close to Veronica, but Sarah and she were tight."

Back in high school, Tim's sister had been a pretty, blonde dynamo all the boys drooled over. She'd died of leukemia while still in college. Until now, Cassidy had forgotten that Veronica and his sister cheered together. Going to sporting events hadn't been part of Cassidy's high school experience.

"I'd forgotten all about them being close."

A shadow slid over his face. "Sarah had lots of friends."

She wasn't sure what made her continue the conversation, other than she found herself wanting to comfort him, yet not sure how. "You must miss her very much."

"I do miss her." A distant look filled his gaze. "Lindsey and I were always the quiet ones. Sarah kept life lively. She'd have loved the twins. I wish they'd had a chance to know her."

Unexpectedly his voice grew thick with emotion and sadness darkened his eyes.

*Way to go, Cassidy*, she told herself.

"I love the names you picked for your girls." Cassidy changed the subject a bit awkwardly. "Where did they come from?"

He blinked and the shadow darkening his eyes disappeared.

"Esther was named for my grandmother." His smile reminded her of the sun appearing from behind a dark cloud. "Gram lives in Phoenix. She's a spunky woman who says what she thinks. Ellyn was named after one of Caro's sorority sisters."

"You picked one name. Caro picked the other."

"Exactly," he confirmed. "Fifty-fifty, right down the middle."

Cassidy thought, but didn't say, that it seemed a bit too calculated for her. But then, what did she know? She didn't have a husband or children. Didn't really see that in her crystal ball for the immediate future.

But she'd gotten Tim's mind off his sister and made him smile. Mission accomplished. Now she just had to keep that sexy smile on those incredible lips. "Is running what you do to relax?"

He nodded and picked up the pace to a jog. "Usually on a treadmill. The girls are too young to leave alone and I prefer not to get a babysitter unless it's absolutely necessary."

"I imagine it's not easy being a single parent."

"I'm luckier than most. My mother took early retirement to help with the girls after Caro died. My dad adores them. Lindsey has playdates with them every week. I also have a neighbor girl who pitches in. Lots of help."

*Lots of help*, Cassidy thought, *but still a lonely journey.*

"Are the girls why you don't date?" It seemed a logical conclusion.

His expression turned serious once again. "It's difficult for me to do anything that takes time away from them."

"What about Jayne?" The question quite simply popped out. Perhaps it had been because the librarian had conveniently run into them at the street dance last week. "I've seen you two out together."

He shook his head. "I don't know why everyone is so determined to throw us together. Jayne and I are friends. Like you and me."

Cassidy strove for neutral. "Do you kiss Jayne like you kissed me?"

Tim began to slow his pace as they approached the lake. "Jayne is like a sister to me."

"I'll take that as a no." Cassidy wondered what madness made her keep pushing for more, for some sort of declaration that he found her sexy in a way he didn't find Jayne.

Hadn't he already made it perfectly clear he didn't want her? Yet, there was a curious energy in the air that even he had to have noticed. Heck, the air practically sizzled whenever they were together. "You don't think of me as a sister."

He smiled, a quick flash of white that had her pulse picking up speed. "You sound pretty sure of that."

"Just to put to bed any doubts…" Cassidy put a finger to her mouth, pulling his attention to her bright red lips and stopped. "I believe a test is in order."

"Test?" His brows pulled together and puzzlement filled his eyes. "What kind of test?"

Abruptly, and without warning, Cassidy wrapped her arms around his neck and pressed her lips to his.

For a second he stood frozen, stiff. Then, thank goodness, his arms slid around her waist and he kissed her back.

Cassidy let herself forget everything except the feel and the taste of him. The arms that held her so tightly were strong and muscular, the lips firm and seductive.

When Tim's tongue swept along her mouth, she parted her lips and he immediately deepened the kiss. The heat that had ignited the second she'd kissed him turned fiery hot. As if he was there to save her from going under a third time, Cassidy tightened her hold on his neck.

Only a thin layer of clothes separated them, but she wanted to be closer, *needed* to be closer. She longed to feel his warm skin beneath her hands, slide her fingers along his muscles, taste the salty—

Tim jerked back and her daydream disappeared in a poof of disappointment.

"Someone's coming," he said in a hoarse whisper.

Because it seemed expected, Cassidy smoothed her shirt. She'd have touched up her lipstick—a smart woman always had a tube with her—but the voices Tim heard were now loud.

Two middle-aged couples, dressed fashionably—for the sixty-plus set—in walking shorts and sturdy shoes, stepped into view.

They looked familiar, at least the women did. But they weren't her customers. If they had been, Cassidy would have remembered them. She had a good memory for the faces and names of her clientele.

"Tim." The other woman uttered his name in a single breath, looking flummoxed.

It was the only word Cassidy could think of to describe the complete and utter shock on the gray-haired woman's face as her gaze shifted from Tim to her. Her companion, a pretty redhead from the bottle, appeared only mildly curious.

"Paula. Emerson." Tim's voice was surprisingly steady. He shifted his gaze to the other couple. "I don't believe we've met."

"These are our old friends, the Lenzes, from our college days." Paula's smile may have been bright, but her gaze, when it landed on Cassidy, turned cool.

Introductions were quickly dispensed with and there were hearty smiles and comments about the invigorating walk and lovely scenery all around. Then Cassidy watched with some amusement as Paula Connors, Jayne's oh-so-proper mama, began to dig for information like a badger going after a tasty rodent.

## Chapter Six

Tim had nearly groaned aloud when Jayne's parents stepped into the clearing. Though he had no qualms about skipping his cousin's wedding to spend the evening with a friend, he knew Jayne's mother would be all over him about his decision.

Jayne and the bride weren't friends, had never been friends, barely knew each other. Still, Paula had intimated the last time he'd seen her that Jayne was simply crushed she hadn't received an invitation to Veronica's wedding. The implication had been clear. He should ask her daughter to the wedding.

But even as Tim had considered the possibility, he knew it wouldn't be fair to Jayne. People in Jackson Hole had already begun to think of them as a couple. How was Jayne ever going to meet someone special if she spent her free time with him?

So he hadn't asked her, even when his own mother had weighed in on the issue. He was exceedingly glad he'd made that decision. Otherwise, he'd have disappointed her by being late. More important, he'd never have been able to ditch the party and take off with Cassidy.

A run in the mountains with a beautiful woman had been just what he'd needed after a precipitous delivery that could have had an unhappy outcome. And he'd be damned if he'd feel guilty about taking a few hours of R & R.

"Don't you agree, Tim darling?"

He jerked his head up. Out of the corner of his eye he saw Cassidy stifle a grin.

"Ah, I missed the question." Tim refused to apologize.

Any sane man's mind would have wandered listening to her extol Jayne's virtues after being forced to jump through a bunch of mental hoops to bring her up to speed on every facet of his past twenty-four hours.

"I said—" Paula's smile remained on her face, but there was an almost imperceptible edge to her voice "—it's quite impressive that Jayne was appointed to the Mayor's Task Force on Truancy and Absenteeism."

"I hadn't heard that," Tim murmured. "Yes, that is impressive. I understand why Tripp chose her. As a media specialist, she's around students all day."

"Dr. Mitzi McGregor is also part of the task force." Confident she now had his full attention, Paula's expression relaxed. "I'm not sure who's the chair."

"I am."

The answer came from beside him.

Tim turned to Cassidy and smiled, delighted with the news. "You didn't tell me."

"Never had a chance." Cassidy turned to Paula. "I don't know Jayne all that well. This will be a good chance for us to get better acquainted."

The other couple had already moved down to the edge of the lake. Emerson squeezed his wife's shoulder. "I'll keep our guests company. Don't be too long."

Paula narrowed her gaze.

"Do you really expect me to believe that you're the *chair* of something so important?" The woman made a scoffing sound. "You didn't even go to college."

"Actually—" Cassidy's voice remained level though her blue eyes had turned frosty "—I received my degree in business just last year."

Paula sniffed. "One of those online schools, no doubt."

"It was nice running into you and Emerson." Tim's tone was now as frosty as Cassidy's eyes. "I believe it's time you tend to your friends."

The woman would have had to be deaf—or stupid— not to hear the dismissal in his tone. Paula Connors was many things; stupid wasn't one of them.

"You're right. I'm being a bad friend. Give your parents my regards." Paula scurried off as fast as her Rockports could carry her, without a single backward glance.

"Good riddance," Tim muttered.

"What do you want to bet she'll be on the phone or texting your mother before we're out of sight?" A mischievous glint danced in Cassidy's eyes.

Tim laughed aloud, the tension from the past few minutes disappearing with the sound. He was barely aware of Paula turning with an assessing air. "That's a bet I'd be destined to lose."

"Matchmaking mamas." Cassidy bent over and stretched, giving him a view of her exceptional backside. She heaved a melodramatic sigh. "What are ya gonna do?"

"Race you to the car." He took off running. He grinned when he heard her footfalls but only increased his speed.

As they ran, the last of the tension eased from his shoulders and he realized that if he ever did have the time to date anyone, it wouldn't be Jayne Connors.

No, if he had the time, the woman would be Cassidy Kaye.

\* \* \*

Cassidy opened a bag of Oreo cookies and dumped some in a bowl before wandering over to where Tim sat, feet plopped on her battered coffee table.

Once they'd reached their vehicles, Cassidy had expected Tim to say no when she invited him over for a dinner of ramen noodle soup and beer. To her surprise, he'd accepted. He must have decided that, since he was already in the doghouse with mama bear, he might as well damn himself further.

When they'd arrived, she gave him a beer then told him to relax and put his feet up. He didn't seem to understand she meant that literally, until she lifted his legs and put his feet on the scarred trunk that doubled as a coffee table in the cramped space.

He appeared to enjoy the soup: ramen noodles jazzed up with cabbage, carrots and cut-up chicken. Dessert, she assured him, wasn't going to be so fancy.

Oreo cookies. Take 'em or leave 'em.

When she sat on the sofa and placed the bowl between them, he took one almost immediately.

"I haven't had one of these in years," he confided.

"Get out of here."

His eyes widened.

"No, I mean, I can't believe you could do without Oreos for so long." Cassidy took one, opened it and let the tip of her tongue swirl around the white center.

His eyes went dark.

She resisted the urge to grin. As she gave the cookie one more swipe, she noted his gaze remained firmly fixed on her mouth. "In my house, Oreos are a staple."

"I wish they were in mine."

"What's stopping you?"

He finished off one cookie and reached for another. "I have to set a good example for the girls."

"Phooey."

He lifted a brow. "Phooey?"

"You don't have to enjoy them at every meal, although that's how I roll." She offered him an impish smile. "But what's the harm in having a cookie for dessert or for a snack once a week? When you can't have something, it can become too important to you later in life."

Cassidy realized that was partly why she was so determined to live every day on her own terms.

"That's a good point." Tim picked up his bottle of beer and took a long pull. His gaze strayed to the wall clock that bore a distinct resemblance to a pepperoni pizza.

Cassidy inhaled sharply. Was he thinking of leaving? That she wouldn't permit. The night was still young and the guy needed some R & R.

"Since you like horror flicks, I thought we could watch *The Fly*." Cassidy kept her voice light knowing if she pressed too hard, he'd bolt. "If you need an extra inducement, I've got Jiffy Pop."

His eyes lit up. "The kind you make on the stove top?"

She nodded.

"*The Fly*. Jiffy Pop. A beautiful woman." Tim rubbed his chin then relaxed against the back of the soft sofa with the red, purple and yellow throw pillows. "I'm in."

*The Fly* ended up to be just as creepy—and hilarious—as Tim remembered. During the course of the movie, he munched on popcorn and Oreos, drank the rest of his beer and got to know Cassidy a little better.

"Are you excited about the task force?" he asked, as the man on the screen began to take on fly-like features. Tim ignored the *help me* cries coming from the small television and focused on Cassidy.

She twirled her bottle of beer between her fingers and her gaze grew thoughtful. "I am. Truancy is a first step down a slippery slope. Kids get behind at school. They fail their classes and end up dropping out. There's nothing waiting for them then other than a life of minimum-wage jobs and poverty."

"It matters to you, what happens to those kids." He could see it in her eyes, hear it in the passion in her voice.

"I grew up one wrong decision away from that kind of life," she told him quite seriously. "There were so many times I thought about taking off. Most of these kids are under tremendous pressures at home. School is the least of their concerns."

"You persevered."

"I wanted more. And, despite what my mom was always telling me, I believed I deserved more." She clenched the hand holding the ice-cold beer to her heart and did her best Scarlett O'Hara impression. "As God is my witness, I will be a success."

Admiration rose inside him for that long-ago girl, for the woman who'd fought so many demons and come out on top.

Without thinking he took the beer from her fingers and placed it on a side table, along with the bowl of cookies, and tugged her to him. "Tripp couldn't have picked a better person to chair that task force."

She winked. "That's what I told him."

Tim laughed, pressed a kiss against her hair. "You're a special woman, Cassidy Kaye."

She gazed into his eyes. "Don't tell me you're only just realizing that?"

He brushed a strand of hair back from her face and found it as soft as silk. "I guess I'm a slow learner."

She wound her arms around his neck and met his gaze. "You have any questions, just ask me. I'm a good teacher."

Their gazes locked. The air took on the consistency of thick whipped cream.

"Are you looking for something serious?" he asked in a quiet tone after an impossibly long moment.

"I'm not." Cassidy kept her gaze steady and lied.

"I don't have any protection." He stopped and gave an embarrassed laugh. "Forgive me. I take too much for granted. I just assumed—"

"You assumed correctly." She would not apologize for wanting him, for needing him tonight. On whatever terms. "I have condoms."

No need to tell him that she'd picked up the box before their Old West Days date. Just in case...

Tim gazed at her beautiful face, at the wide mouth usually tipped in a smile. How he wanted her beneath him.

He hadn't made love since Caro died. He'd thought the desire for a woman's touch had died with his wife. But now, feeling Cassidy's body pressed against him and his own response to her closeness told him every part of him was very much alive.

She slipped her hands under his shirt, gripping the edges of the fabric with her fingers, and tugged it upward. "How about we get more—"

Cassidy inhaled sharply.

His hands were on her skin, sliding up her sides toward her aching breasts, the tips of his fingers leaving a wake of heat wherever they touched. The clasp of her bra opened easily and her breasts spilled into his waiting palms.

When his thumbs scraped across the aching tips of her nipples, she went wet.

Forget Oreos. This was the best dessert ever.

He pushed her shirt out of the way and lowered his head. His breath fanned her skin as his tongue circled her...

The jarring ring from the phone he'd placed on the trunk had Tim jerking back.

"Let it go to voice mail," Cassidy urged, leaning forward, her tongue sliding up his neck.

He was tempted. Very tempted. But in his practice, they delivered their own babies while they were in town.

"Can't." Swearing softly under his breath, he reached for his phone and clicked on. "Dr. Duggan."

"Tim."

He briefly closed his eyes, bit back a groan. He should have paid attention to the ringtone. "Yes, Mom."

"You sound different. Everything okay?"

"Everything is fine. How are the girls?"

"They're wonderful. They loved the wedding, but they're missing their daddy."

"Something came up." Deliberately he kept his response brief. Past experience told him, give his mother an inch, she'd take the whole damn ball field.

"Paula called me. She told me—"

"Is there a point to this call, Mother?"

There was a long pause on the other end. "You're with her now, aren't you?"

"I'll pick up the twins from Sunday school tomorrow as we planned—" he began, determined to get off the phone as quickly as possible.

"No," his mother continued, speaking quickly as if fearing he might end the call. "You need to pick them up now."

"Now?"

"Right now."

"Why?"

"Your father isn't feeling well. I think he might be coming down with something," she said in a hurried tone. "I think it best you pick them up right now so we can go to bed."

"What symptoms is Dad having?" Tim straightened on the sofa. Though his voice came out cool and composed, this was his *father*. His heart slammed against his ribs.

As if sensing the growing tension, Cassidy sat back. Concern replaced passion in her blue eyes.

"Any chest pain? Have you taken his blood pressure? Checked his pulse?" He fired off the questions.

Last year his father had developed an irregular heart rhythm, the cause of which no cardiologist had been able to pin down despite extensive testing. They'd put him on some medications and he'd appeared to be doing well.

*Until tonight.*

"No chest pain and his blood pressure is fine," Suzanne reassured him. "I believe he's simply tired. I think he overdid it with the yard work this afternoon. And keeping track of two high-spirited girls at a reception when you're sixty years old is no easy task."

The well-aimed zinger hit the target. But hadn't his mother insisted she wanted to take the girls? Show them off? Still, he *had* promised to be there.

He took a deep breath and let it out slowly. The weight of responsibility had never been so heavy. "I'll be right there."

"Good."

Ignoring the satisfaction in his mother's voice, Tim said goodbye and hung up.

Giving Cassidy's shoulder a squeeze, he stood up. "I need to go."

She fastened her bra, adjusted her shirt before slowly pulling to her feet. "Is your dad okay?"

"I think so." Warmed by her concern, he brushed a kiss across her cheek. "Sounds like he just overdid it today. But I'll check him out when I pick up the girls."

Her brows pulled together. "I thought they were spending the night."

"I did, too." He shrugged, knowing he needed to go, but strangely reluctant to leave her. "Plans apparently have changed."

"Happens all the time," she said with a rueful smile, then grabbed his face and planted a hard kiss on his lips.

She took a step back and expelled a heavy sigh. "Now, get out of here before I decide to lock the door and not play nice."

## Chapter Seven

"Tim said something about you not feeling well." Lindsey Taylor, Tim's younger sister, shoved a bowl of whipped potatoes into his hands and glanced worriedly at their father.

"Just my knee." Steve Duggan gave a dismissive wave. "Couple of ibuprofen and I was as good as new."

On the drive over to his parents' home last night, Tim had begun to wonder if his father's health was simply a ruse designed to get him out of Cassidy's "lair" and back where his mother thought he belonged.

His suspicions were confirmed when his father had met him at the door. When Tim had asked how he felt, his dad had laughed ruefully and said he was fine. Other than that the knee he'd injured skiing years ago was sore after so much dancing.

His mother hadn't bothered to look apologetic. When she'd blithely told him the twins could stay the night after all, Tim had been so angry he hadn't replied. Instead, he'd grabbed the girls' overnight bags. Ignoring their howls of protest, he had taken them home.

Though sorely tempted to skip Sunday dinner with the family, Tim knew Lindsey and Zach would be there. His sister and her husband had been in Denver seeing friends. All week Esther and Ellyn had been looking forward to seeing their aunt and uncle.

For that reason alone, Tim had put aside his irritation over his mother's connivance.

"How was the wedding?" Zach took the bowl of whipped potatoes from Tim. "We'd hoped to get back for it, but the plane had mechanical issues. We didn't get in until after eleven."

"I've told Lindsey many times she needs to schedule flights earlier in the—"

"I made the reservations." Zach didn't wait for Suzanne to finish. "Taking an earlier flight didn't work with our schedule."

Tim silently applauded his brother-in-law. His mother faced a formidable adversary in the high school football coach. Zach was fiercely protective of his wife. He'd set the tone from the beginning, making it clear to Suzanne that he wouldn't tolerate her disparaging Lindsey.

His mother opened her mouth, appeared to think better of whatever she'd been about to say and closed it without speaking.

"Thanks for bringing the corn salad, Aunt Lindsey." Ellyn gave her aunt a gap-toothed smile. "I told Daddy I hoped, I hoped, I hoped, you'd bring it today."

"It's my favorite." Esther picked a Fritos chip off the top of hers and popped it into her mouth.

"Mine, too," Ellyn echoed.

Tim's heart swelled with love as his gaze settled on his daughters' sweet faces. Then he winced. This morning the girls had begged him to put their hair in pigtails. Though

Tim had given it his best shot, he noticed he hadn't quite gotten them even.

His mother took a sip of her iced tea and, obviously sensing the conversation about flight scheduling was a dead end, refocused on Tim.

Before she even opened her mouth, Tim saw where she was headed. His gaze met hers. *Don't go there*, he silently warned.

"Did your brother tell you he spent last evening with Cassidy Kaye?" Suzanne tossed out the comment then daintily began buttering a sourdough bun.

"I didn't realize you and Cassidy were dating," Lindsey said with undisguised delight.

"She cuts my hair," Zach informed him. "She's an interesting woman. How long have you two been together?"

"They're not dating." Suzanne practically shouted the words. When everyone turned to her in mild alarm, she visibly pulled herself together. "I simply meant that for some reason, instead of spending the evening at his cousin's wedding, Tim chose to spend it elsewhere."

Her gaze shifted to Lindsey. "And *you* were out of town."

To Tim's surprise, his sister simply laughed. Though their mother's comments usually got Lindsey's back up, it appeared that today, not even her mother's caustic comments could quash her upbeat mood.

If that was what a week in Denver accomplished, Tim decided he needed a Colorado vacation.

"What's put a bee in your bonnet?" Lindsey's tone was almost teasing. "Veronica was always Sarah's friend, not ours."

A look of sadness crossed Suzanne's face. Even though it had been over a decade since Sarah had died and they all felt her loss, no one felt it more acutely than Suzanne.

Of her three children, Sarah had been Suzanne's favorite and a source of endless pride.

Lindsey gazed down at the glob of gravy on her whipped potatoes and for a second turned green. Looking away, she took a sip of water and appeared to settle. "All I'm saying is it's not like Veronica would care whether Tim or I was there."

Suzanne blinked back tears. "I cared."

Thankfully, the girls were too involved with flipping corn chips at each other to notice the tremble in their grandmother's voice. Normally, Tim would have reprimanded his daughters for playing with food. This time, he was grateful they were occupied.

"Ah, honey." His dad reached over but Suzanne shook off his hand.

"A *family* event," she said with added emphasis. "And neither my son nor my daughter deigned to show up."

"That's not fair, Suzanne." Zach's voice held a warning.

"Okay, you and Lindsey get a pass," Suzanne conceded before her gaze shifted.

Tim kept his eyes steady on hers. "If I'd been with Jayne you wouldn't have cared if I missed the reception."

"I could understand that behavior," his mother admitted. "But Cassidy Kaye? Really, Timothy, what were you thinking?"

He was spared from answering when a cat with a dark head, white body and raccoon-like tail leaped onto the table.

Suzanne jumped up so quickly only her husband's fast hand saved her water glass from tumbling over.

Undisturbed, the cat glanced around, saw the bread basket and batted a bun from the stack with one swipe.

Suzanne gasped, shrieked. "Get him off the table, Steve."

Her husband reached for the cat, who backed out of reach, almost upsetting the gravy boat.

The girls giggled.

Tim knew he should help but instead sat back in his chair, enjoying the show.

His sister rolled her eyes then rose and scooped up the animal, cuddling him against her chest. "Poor sweet kitty," she crooned. "Did they scare you?"

The cat's tail swished back and forth, and Tim swore the animal gave his mother a smug smile. He took in the dark head, the white body and the striped tail. He turned to his father. "Is that Runt?"

"He's now known as Domino." Steve stifled a smile as his wife made a shooing motion at her daughter, apparently not content to have the cat simply off the table. "The boy needed a proper name."

"I thought you weren't going to keep him." Ignoring the chaos, Tim took a sip of wine.

"We're still working on finding him a home." Steve gazed speculatively at his son and lifted a brow.

Tim raised a hand. "We've been down this road. Perhaps when the girls are older."

"Taking the cat home might soften up your mother."

Tim watched Suzanne usher out Lindsey and the cat. He took a contemplative sip of wine then shook his head. "Nothing will ever change her mind about Cassidy."

"You need to follow your heart, son."

Tim looked at his father in surprise. "Cassidy and I are simply friends. I doubt I'll be seeing her again."

"That surprises me," Steve said.

"That I won't be seeing her again?"

"That you'd let your mother dictate your actions."

Before Tim could protest that wasn't it at all, the women returned without the cat. Calm descended over the table and Cassidy wasn't brought up again.

For Cassidy, the next few weeks sped by like a locomotive on crack. Every person in Jackson Hole seemed determined to get their hair cut before Independence Day. In addition, Cassidy had now done wedding hair three weeks in a row.

Hallelujah, she had this evening free. Unfortunately, she'd been too busy working to line anything up with her friends.

This morning she'd colored her hair a rich chocolate brown with burnished gold highlights. Because she liked to coordinate hair with clothes, she slipped into a recent consignment store "find," a vintage-style gold-and-brown floral dress with spaghetti straps and a scooped neck. The colors and style might be more subdued than what she normally wore but it suited her mood this evening.

No doubt about it. She looked incredible.

*All dressed up with nowhere to go.*

Not entirely true. Wally's Place was always an option. There would be friends enjoying the live band or playing a game of darts. Heck, she might even hike up her skirts and ride the bull again.

For some reason the thought held little appeal without Tim there to cheer her on. She longed to see him again but that wasn't going to happen.

Always the perfect gentleman, Tim had called the day after Veronica's wedding. He'd thanked her for the dinner, the Oreos and the run. He hadn't mentioned the make-out session on the sofa. Or getting together again.

They'd both known whatever there was between them was destined for a short run, she thought philosophically. They led busy lives. His revolved around home and family. Hers revolved around growing her business.

She was an independent woman and very capable of entertaining herself. Cassidy considered her options. Perfect Pizza had a new cream-cheese-and-pineapple pizza she'd been dying to try. She'd grab a slice and go from there.

After satisfying her hunger cravings and running one

little errand, she would check out the action at Wally's Place. If there was nothing going on, she'd come home, kick off her cowboy boots and cuddle up to *Glory in Death*.

Because as every woman knew, the next best thing to a man in your bed was a good book.


After dropping Esther and Ellyn off at a friend's house for a birthday sleepover, Tim automatically steered the car in the direction of home. As he pulled to a stop at the intersection where he should turn, he abruptly changed direction.

Instead of eating leftover casserole, he'd pick up a pizza. *Then* he'd head home, put up his feet and relax while enjoying a slice of pepperoni. Maybe he'd watch a movie. There was a new horror flick out he wanted to see.

The thought brought back memories of *The Fly* and that last night with Cassidy. An evening he'd enjoyed immensely.

Tim pulled into a parking spot down the street from Perfect Pizza and got out. He liked Cassidy, liked her a lot in fact. But he could see himself getting too involved, too serious, too quickly. Marriage wasn't in his game plan.

Having two daughters and a busy career left little time for anything else. He wasn't one of those guys who could do it all. Caro had always accused him of not having enough time for family. Looking back, he could see she was right. He would not let another woman down.

Cassidy was beautiful, intelligent and sexy. The spirited entrepreneur deserved to be with a guy who could offer her more than a fling. But she had to be someone who wouldn't try to change her, who wouldn't want to squeeze her into some square box.

Stepping inside the door of Perfect Pizza, Tim paused and inhaled deeply, letting the enticing scent of spices, tomato and garlic envelope him.

"Tim."

Before he could turn fully, he was enveloped in a hug.

"Lindsey." Genuine pleasure laced his words. "I didn't expect to see you here."

His sister was a pretty woman with blue-green eyes and hair the color of burnished bronze. Tonight, she glowed. After years of living in her sister's shadow, she'd come into her own in recent years. It was obvious she was content with her life and happy in her marriage.

"Join us. We have a table and our pizza should be out any second." Before she even finished speaking, Lindsey looped her arm through his and pulled him into the dining area.

"I don't want to crash your date night."

"You're not crashing," she said. "Neither is Cassidy."

Tim's senses went on high alert. "Cassidy?"

"She came in by herself. We invited her to join us."

Cassidy looked up and smiled when he reached the table. "Hey, Tim."

"Hey, Cass." Though he told himself to play it cool, when her smiling blue eyes met his, he grinned.

An hour later, Tim had eaten way too much pizza and talked way too much. That was Lindsey's fault. She'd always had a way of drawing him out.

Cassidy shared that same talent. No wonder they seemed to get along so well.

"Enough shop talk." Tim raised a hand when Lindsey asked him another question about pregnancy, of all things. Though he was grateful for her interest in his practice, he didn't want to monopolize the conversation. "You said earlier you were here celebrating. But I know it's not your anniversary."

Lindsey exchanged a look with her husband.

Cassidy took a sip of soda and angled her head.

"We want to keep this our little secret for now, so you

have to promise not to tell anyone." Lindsey's gaze shifted between him and Cassidy.

When they both agreed, his sister took a deep breath and grabbed her husband's hand. "We're pregnant."

"Ohmigod." Cassidy squealed then flung her arms around Lindsey's neck. "Congratulations."

Tim raked a hand through his hair. He'd expected this announcement eventually but the realization still left him slightly off balance.

"My kid sister is having a baby," he murmured. "I can't believe it."

"Aren't you happy for us?"

Hearing the hurt in Lindsey's voice, Tim pulled himself together and grasped her hands tightly in his. "Extremely happy. You and Zach will be great parents. The girls will love having a baby cousin to spoil."

"We're over the moon," Zach admitted, a smile lifting his lips. "We've decided to wait until after the first trimester to make the announcement."

The OB in Tim surfaced. "Have you seen a doctor?"

"I saw Travis last week," his sister said, referring to Tim's partner, Dr. Travis Fisher. "He said my hormone levels are right where they should be and the heartbeat is strong."

"If I'd have known you were celebrating, I wouldn't have intruded," Cassidy said.

"Me, either," Tim added.

Lindsey gripped one of Cassidy's hands then squeezed Tim's. "I wanted so much to share the news. Having you both here gave me that chance. But remember..."

His sister released their hands and mimed zipping her lips.

"What about Mom?" Tim asked. "Have you told her and Dad the good news?"

"I want to tell her." Lindsey spoke haltingly. "But..."

When his wife's lips began to tremble, Zach reached over and took her hand.

"You know how she can be. She'll only magnify my fears with her own worries." Lindsey's eyes beseeched him to understand.

Tim zipped his lips shut. "Sealed."

"Double sealed with duct tape," Cassidy said and made Lindsey smile.

They talked a little while longer before his sister began to yawn. Zach insisted they call it a night. After a flurry of hugs and well-wishes, the happy couple departed, leaving Cassidy and Tim alone at the table.

Cassidy immediately began rummaging in her bag, pulling out a few crumpled bills and adding them to the tip Zach had left.

"I suppose I should head home, too." But, like Cassidy, Tim remained seated.

Cassidy clucked her tongue. "You realize, Doogie, that going home at eight o'clock on a Friday night is pretty pathetic?"

He angled his head. "You got something better in mind?"

"Not really." She gave a little chuckle. "I have to run a quick errand, so my night is looking almost as pathetic as yours."

"Want company?"

When she shot him a curious look, he lifted a shoulder in a slight shrug. "Might as well have a boring evening together. What do you say?"

She stared at him for a long moment then grinned, a devilish gleam in her eyes. "What the hell. If you can't live dangerously, what's the point?"

Tim and Cassidy stepped out of Perfect Pizza into a warm June evening. They strolled down the sidewalk, he in jeans and sneakers and Cassidy in a flouncy dress with matching cowboy boots. In the shimmering light, the streaks in her hair reminded him of spun gold.

There were some women—like his mother and Jayne—who rarely changed their clothing style or hair. Then there was Cassidy, who changed hers almost daily. He liked the variety and the way she rocked a dozen different looks.

"What's the errand?" he asked when she gestured for them to turn south at the corner.

"A client left her wallet at the salon. It's difficult for her to get around, so I said I'd drop it off."

When Cassidy gave the street name, he nearly flinched. But he schooled his features, remembering the area commonly considered the "wrong side of the tracks" was also where she'd grown up. "That's nice of you to do this for her."

She waved a dismissive hand, her glittery nails dancing in the light. "Anyone would do the same."

Tim considered her words, nodded. "That's what I like about Jackson Hole. Everyone helps each other. I'm trying to teach my girls to be good neighbors and friends."

"You mentioned they're at a birthday party this evening?"

"A sleepover." He shook his head. "When did they get so big?"

Cassidy slanted a sideways glance. "Since you have the entire night free, I'm surprised you're not with Jayne."

Perhaps because he'd had this discussion earlier with his mother, Tim's temper spiked. "Why does everyone persist in thinking I'm attracted to Jayne when I've made it clear we're only friends?"

Anger and irritation simmered beneath the words but Cassidy only smiled.

"In my case, it's probably because I'm still getting to know you." Cassidy sounded almost cheerful now. "It's difficult to really get to know a person, because most of the conversations people have tend to be superficial."

"True. Even when we ask questions, we often don't listen to the answer."

Flashes of blue, yellow and pink at his feet caught his eye. He glanced down and realized it was Monopoly money. A favorite game of his growing up. "What games did you play as a child?"

Cassidy chuckled as if he'd made a joke.

"I'm serious." Without his gaze leaving her face, he kicked a basketball from the sidewalk back into a weed-strewn yard. At her continued silence, he gestured with one hand. "Think of it as a question to help us become more intimately acquainted."

He wasn't sure why he'd included the word *intimately*. Yet, there it was, hanging in the air between them.

"If intimacy is your goal, I know lots of ways you and I can become more intimately acquainted and not a single one has to do with games." She placed a glitter-tipped finger against her mouth. "Though perhaps it might be fun to incorporate a game or two…"

Tim laughed. Trust Cassidy to put her own spin on an innocent question. "Just answer."

An odd look filled her eyes. "You first."

Because of the money strewn across the sidewalk, Monopoly came first to mind. But almost immediately, another memory surfaced. "Word-find games."

Cassidy's brows pulled together. "Come again?"

"You know, where you have a whole page of letters and hidden words are embedded." Tim smiled, remembering. "My mother would make up four sheets appropriate to each of our reading levels every week. She'd time us. Five minutes per page. Whoever found the most words in the time allotted would win the round. After four rounds, the overall winner was chosen."

Instead of teasing him about always winning—which was true—Cassidy hesitated. "Your mother did that? Every week?"

Tim shot her a puzzled look.

"That took a lot of work. I mean, there were three of you."

"You're right." He heard surprise in his own voice. In his anger over her meddling, it was easy to forget everything his mother had done—and continued to do—for her family.

There was no time to say more as Cassidy came to an abrupt halt in front of a ramshackle white house with peeling paint, ripped-off shingles and a yard without a single blade of grass.

She took a tattered wallet from her bag and shoved it into his hands. "Hold this a sec."

Her hand dived back into the bag the size of Texas and came out with a twenty. She took the wallet back from him and slipped the bill inside. Cassidy's grin flashed. "I don't know anyone who doesn't like a surprise."

With a sexy sway to her hips, Cassidy sashayed up to the crumbling front stoop and rang the bell. After several minutes a gray-haired woman opened the door, leaning heavily on a walker.

Cassidy smiled and chatted for a minute, waved away the woman's effusive thanks before returning to Tim.

"Time to get the hell out of Dodge." Though the night air was warm, she shivered. "This neighborhood holds too many bad memories. And, no, I don't want to talk about any of them."

"Okay," he said agreeably. "We'll go back to our game discussion."

"That works for me." She angled her head. "What other games did you play?"

"Good try. It's your turn."

Her smile vanished. "Pass."

"Your turn," he repeated.

"Hide-and-seek," she said after a lengthy silence.

The game had been a favorite of his younger sisters. "That can be fun."

"Maybe in your house," she muttered.

"What did you say?"

"Yes, loads of fun." She picked up the pace, taking long strides down the walk as if trying to distance herself from something. The area? Or memories?

He caught up with her and took her hand, surprised at how cold it felt. "Tell me about your games of hide-and-seek."

"In my house it wasn't a game—it was life-and-death." She gave a halfhearted laugh. "That's how it felt, anyway."

The darkness that surrounded them created an aura of intimacy. "Tell me."

Tim listened as she spoke haltingly of her mother's boyfriends and how they'd want her to sit on their laps. How they'd stroke her blond hair and tell her how pretty she was...

His heart slammed against his ribs. "Did they ever—"

Cassidy shook her head. "I got really good at hiding."

"Thank God." He exhaled a breath. "Where was your mother while this was going on?"

"High. Drunk. Both."

The words were said so matter-of-factly, as if such occurrences were nothing unusual. Sympathy for the young girl who'd had to endure so much rose inside him as well as a healthy dose of anger directed at her worthless mother.

"That's why I'm excited to lead this task force." Cassidy's expression changed from pensive to determined. "I understand how challenges at home affect school success. I'm excited to come up with concrete recommendations on what the community and the school district can do to help."

"Tripp is lucky to have you," he said. "You're an amazing woman, Cassidy Kaye."

She gazed at him through lowered lashes. "Why did it take you this long to realize something so obvious?"

## *Chapter Eight*

On the walk back to her apartment, Tim took Cassidy's hand as they continued to discuss everything from mutual friends to movies that would be coming out in the next few weeks. Why couldn't it be like this with other men?

With Tim, everything was easy. She could talk to him about anything and know he would never betray her confidence. She could be herself and feel accepted. And then there was the sizzle.

None of the guys she'd dated had elicited such lust. Simply holding his hand sent shivers of desire sliding up and down her spine.

But Tim had made it perfectly clear—both in actions and words—that while he was sexually attracted to her, he wasn't looking for anything long-term.

The fact that she was considering sleeping with him despite these stipulations made her wonder if she was turning into her mother, a woman men used but never loved.

The instant the thought struck, she tossed it. This wasn't the same at all. Unlike her mother, *she* was self-aware.

*No.* She shook her head. It wasn't the same at all.

"No?" Tim angled his head. "You really wouldn't have tried it?"

With sex on the brain, Cassidy had listened with only half an ear to Tim's experience eating octopus at a medical convention last year.

She flushed, grateful only one word of her scattered thoughts had slipped past her lips. Cassidy wrinkled her nose. "Okay, yes. It sounds gross but honestly, I'd have tried it, too. Just to see if a creature with eight arms really does taste like Colonel Sanders."

The comment made Tim laugh.

Casually, Cassidy wrapped her fingers around his arm as they climbed the stairs to her unit. Once she unlocked the door, her heart began to pound.

From the question in his eyes, she saw he'd also done some thinking on their stroll to her apartment. He wouldn't ask to come in, but he wouldn't refuse an invitation.

Getting naked with him would be playing with fire. But really, what was wrong with a little heat every now and then?

With her pulse now a swift, tripping beat, Cassidy crooked her finger and beckoned in a high, tinny voice, "Step into my parlor, said the spider to the fly."

He laughed aloud. "Stop, already, with the fly references."

Tim was still chuckling as he followed her into the small living space, pulling the door shut behind him. The spark in his hazel eyes gave her a pleasurable jolt and reaffirmed that she wasn't the only one eager to get singed.

"It's been a long time." The huskiness in his voice made her heart lurch.

"For me, too," Cassidy admitted.

He cocked his head questioningly.

"Darn job," she said and they both laughed.

Then he slipped his fingers into her hair and the laughter died in her throat.

The kiss he placed on her mouth was warm and sweet. "I like you, Cassidy."

She twined her hands around his neck. They now stood so close she could feel the hard length of him against her belly. "I like you, too."

"Is that enough?" His voice was soft, reaching inside to a raw, tender place.

Cassidy knew what Tim was asking, what he wanted her to confirm. There would be no words of love. No promises of forever. What they would share tonight would simply be sex.

She wondered why she still hesitated. What could possibly be wrong with spending several pleasurable hours with a sexy man she liked and desired who liked and desired her?

"Of course it's enough." Cassidy took his hand and gave it a tug. "Let's get naked."

When they reached the doorway to her bedroom, he gave her a long, hard kiss, then stepped back, smug satisfaction in his eyes. "I've wanted to do that all evening."

"And I wanted to do this." She planted an openmouthed kiss at the base of his throat, tasting the salt of his skin. "Yep. You really do taste as good as you smell."

Tim gave a self-conscious-sounding laugh even as his hands settled on her backside and he began trailing kisses up her neck.

"I'm serious." She tried to remember how to breathe as he nibbled on her ear. "Did I mention I find you incredibly sexy?"

"You're the sexy one," he murmured. "Beautiful face. Gorgeous legs. And the hair—"

"—That can be any color," she managed to sputter as desire flamed, "on any given day."

"All part of the appeal," Tim asserted. "You're unique, one of a kind. Like no one else."

She smiled, touched by the sentiment.

"And then there are your other, ah, rather impressive attributes." He cleared his throat as his gaze dropped to her chest.

Under his heated stare, her breasts began to tingle, already anticipating the feel of his warm lips.

"They're even more impressive with nothing covering them," Cassidy confided in a throaty whisper.

Though still filled with heat, his hazel eyes twinkled. "I've always been the kind of guy who likes to check out such things firsthand."

"I'm the same way." Cassidy's eyes, which seemed to suddenly develop a mind of their own, zeroed in on the area directly below his waist. "What say we both take a little look-see?"

The sound of ragged breaths and laughter filled the air as they raced to see who could undress the fastest.

Out of the corner of her eye, Cassidy saw Tim's shirt hit the floor. She paused in the midst of her own undressing to admire his bare chest. The man had an athlete's build.

She was seized with an overpowering urge to run her hands over his body, to feel the coiled strength of skin and muscle sliding under her fingers. She wanted him to touch her in the same way, wanted to feel the weight of his body on hers. Wanted to feel him inside her.

When he caught her looking, he responded with a long stare that fried every brain cell she possessed. She worked on her stuck zipper with renewed determination. Cassidy gave a hard tug. Then another. It wouldn't budge. She let out a hiss of frustration.

"Allow me." Tim spun her around and kissed the part

of her bare back already exposed. His warm, moist breath against her skin had her inhaling sharply.

"You're the one who tastes as good as you smell," he said in a husky whisper. He struggled with the zipper for several seconds before it finally slid down.

Cool air flooded her back as the dress parted. In a deft move Tim unclasped her bra then eased the scrap of lace and the dress off her shoulders. The garments dropped to pool at her feet.

Now down to cowboy boots and purple lace panties, Cassidy impetuously struck a centerfold pose, offering Tim an enticing view of her voluptuous body.

"Wow." His eyes widened as his gaze traveled all the way down before moving back up to linger on her magnificent breasts. "Double wow."

Cassidy hefted the objects of his admiration into her hands and jiggled them slightly. "Like what you see?"

Playing with fire, she decided, could be quite fun.

"I like what I see very much." His voice was a husky caress.

Her stomach performed another series of flutters. Cassidy had spent most of her young adult life alternately embracing or discounting her sensuality. When she'd been very young, her ample breasts had been a curse. But seeing the look of admiration in Tim's eyes made her glad for her size Ds.

"You don't have to only look," she told him when he simply continued to stare. "You can touch."

He gave a strangled laugh. "Trust me. I intend to do a lot more than touch."

Without another word, he stepped close and gently tugged her to him. Leaning his forehead against hers, he spoke in a hoarse whisper. "I will make this good for you."

"Promises. Promises." Cassidy kept her tone teasing in a futile attempt to stanch the emotion swelling in her chest.

"So you're saying it's put-up-or-shut-up time?"

The laughter in his voice made her smile. She twined her arms around his neck. "Something like that."

His hand flattened against her lower back, drawing her up against the length of his body. Cassidy pressed herself fully against him. Then his lips were on hers and he was kissing her, long, passionate kisses that rocked her world and left her shaky and off balance. Seconds later the rest of their clothes found a place on the floor.

He continued to kiss her while maneuvering her backward. When her knees came into contact with the mattress, he gave her a slight push.

Cassidy tumbled back, taking him with her. She quickly found herself flat on her back with his hands bracketing her body. A position that suited her just fine.

With eyes the color of Kentucky whiskey, Tim gazed at her. "Now I have you just where I want you."

A smoldering heat flared through Cassidy, a sensation she didn't bother to fight. She gazed up at him through her heavily mascara-coated lashes. "What a coincidence. I was thinking the same thing."

Tim chuckled. Lowering his head, he nuzzled her neck before his mouth began a downward descent. His tongue traced her collarbone even as his smattering of chest hair teased her nipples with every movement.

With deliberate slowness, he brushed his lips across the tip of her breast, the barest hint of friction sending shivers and tingles through her body. Heat flowed through Cassidy's veins like molten lava. His tongue began circling the tip then backing off.

"Please," she moaned.

With a wicked laugh, he finally drew her right nipple into his mouth and suckled while rolling the left tip between his thumb and forefinger.

Fiery arrows of heat shot straight to her core. Cassidy closed her eyes and arched back, moaning softly.

"Look at me," Tim urged in a voice so deep and gravelly it didn't sound like him at all.

She did as he asked, her lashes fluttering open just in time to see him heft her breasts into his hands. They were so big they spilled from his large palms.

"Your skin is like alabaster, so smooth and unmarred. This—" his tongue flicked over the tip as she watched "—reminds me of a sweet peach. I can't help wanting to taste."

Seeing his head lower and his mouth fasten over one tip was incredibly erotic…and a dream come true. He took his time, feasting on one before moving to the other.

Her legs were spread wide beneath him and she felt his hardness against her belly. She bucked upward. "I want you inside me."

"Soon," he promised then his mouth began moving downward again.

He planted openmouthed kisses across her belly, circled her navel with his tongue and made her shiver with desire.

It wasn't until his head dipped again that she realized where he was headed. In her life Cassidy had only been with two men. While they'd been eager to have her satisfy them, neither had given much thought to pleasuring her.

She squirmed. "You don't need to—"

But when his hot breath fanned her most intimate of areas, Cassidy forgot what she'd been about to say.

Tim suckled gently on the warm, moist folds of skin, then his tongue took over. The sensations he drew from her were like nothing she'd experienced before and her body responded with breathtaking speed.

She tried to hold on, to make the pleasure last, but it had been too long and the storm raging inside her was too powerful. Her entire body constricted and released. She cried out as the orgasm ripped through her.

A moment later she lay panting. Aftershocks rippled through her, making her tremble. "I didn't know," she babbled. "I never thought—"

"We're not done yet." Tim caught her mouth and kissed her with a slow thoroughness that soon turned urgent and fevered.

The heat in her lower belly once again became a pulsing need. His fingers stroked and teased, and when he placed one finger inside her, then two, she moaned and pushed upward against his palm.

Sweat beaded Tim's brow and his hair was a rumpled mass. Through the haze of mounting desire, Cassidy heard the tear of foil. Then the hard length was at her entrance, teasing her, moving an inch or two in and then out, as if making sure that she was ready for him.

*Ready?* Her blood was a river of fire in her veins. Her pulse throbbed hard and thick. If he didn't give her more soon, she was going to perish from desire.

Her breath came out in a rush as she found the word she'd been searching for through the fog. She strained upward. "More."

Tim smiled and pushed deeper, filling her completely. In a rhythm as old as time, he began to move in and out. In and out.

"Wrap your legs around me," he ordered, his voice low and guttural.

The second she did, he began to thrust with an almost primal need. Heat radiated from him, urgent and hungry.

Her body vibrated as Tim raced with her, beat for crazed beat. Just when she thought the bliss couldn't be any more intense, he shifted slightly and hit her sweet spot.

Cassidy arched back and came, crying out his name.

Not until he seemed certain that he'd wrung every last

ounce of pleasure from her did he take his own release. He plunged deep in one final thrust, a savage sound of triumph bursting from his lips.

Then he collapsed on her, a well-muscled mass of male. They lay like that for a long moment, bodies slick with sweat, just listening to each other's ragged breathing.

Why had she not known, she thought hazily, that this much satisfaction existed in the world?

Tim drew air slowly into his lungs. "That was…"

"Adequate?" Cassidy offered, determined to keep it light.

Tim lifted his head and smiled, a crooked, boyish grin that melted her heart. "Incredible."

Still going for studied nonchalance, Cassidy gave him a swift kiss. "Yep. Incredible."

After a second, he rolled off her. But instead of hopping out of bed as she expected, he pulled her close. It was almost as if he, too, was reluctant to give up the intimacy.

"Do you want to get up?" he asked when she shifted position slightly to accommodate him next to her.

She hesitated, hedged. "I'm liking where I am right now. What about you?"

He gathered her even closer and kissed her temple. "With the girls at a sleepover, I don't have to rush home. And I don't have any patients due to deliver."

"A whole night off."

"It happens so rarely I'm not sure how to act," he said with a half laugh.

She thought of the pressures he faced every day, the struggle to balance his medical practice with family obligations. "Being a single parent can't be easy."

"Easier than being married," Tim murmured, twining a strand of her hair loosely around his fingers.

He stopped, as if realizing what he'd just admitted.

Cassidy was certain he'd misspoke. Everyone in Jackson Hole knew Tim and Caro had been blissfully happy.

He expelled a breath and spoke into the silence. "I wasn't a good husband."

"What makes you think that?" She kept her tone conversational.

"When you get out of residency and fellowship and join a practice, you have to build your patient base." A shadow passed over his face. "But Caro was home every day with two little ones. I should have understood she needed more support."

"How old were the girls when their mother died?" she asked after several heartbeats of silence.

"Three. They were barely in preschool." Tim sat upright so abruptly Cassidy gave a yelp of surprise.

He swung his legs over the side of the bed but remained seated. His chest rose and fell as he visibly fought for composure.

"Tim," she said softly.

When he gazed at her, she clasped his hand in hers. "Lie back down. Just for a little longer. Please."

He closed his eyes for a brief second then settled back beside her.

"Tell me what has you so tied in knots." She kept her voice low and soothing and tentatively began to stroke his arm.

Though he didn't utter a word, pain filled the stillness.

"Or don't tell me. That's okay, too."

Cassidy understood all too well the desire to hold painful memories close. She respected a person's right to privacy. But she also knew how much better she'd felt earlier after sharing a glimpse of her childhood pain with him.

"We'd been arguing a lot those last couple of months." He blew out a breath. "Nothing we couldn't have gotten through. We were tired. Ellyn had been fighting an ear infection and wasn't sleeping well. Which meant we weren't getting much, either."

Cassidy continued to stroke his arm.

"The world was raining babies and the practice was still a doctor short. We were all putting in long hours." He met Cassidy's gaze. "I told Caro we'd hire a nanny, but she didn't want a stranger in the house. She wanted me. I was their father."

"What about her mother? Or yours?"

"Caro's mother lived out of state and mine was still teaching full-time." Tim's expression grew distant and she could see he was looking back. "That night, I was running late. One of my pregnant patients had showed up in crisis right as I was ready to leave."

Cassidy nodded encouragingly and he continued.

"On the way home I picked up a dozen roses. An apology for being late."

"Were roses Caro's favorite?"

He didn't respond and Cassidy wondered if he'd heard her.

"The instant I stepped into the house, I remembered the cupcakes. The twins had a preschool party the next day and I was supposed to stop at the bakery on my way home. The one thing she'd asked of me and I'd forgotten."

"At least you brought flowers." Cassidy kept her tone light.

"Caro tossed them to the floor. Ellyn was screaming at the top of her lungs. Esther was drawing on herself with magic markers." Tim briefly closed his eyes.

Cassidy could see the scene quite clearly. She shuddered.

"I offered to go back and get the cupcakes, but Caro said she'd do it. Since she had to do everything else herself, why should this be any different?" Emotion made his voice heavy and thick.

Cassidy's heart ached for him. For Caro. For the little girls without a mother.

"Her car was hit two blocks from the house." He took a deep breath, then let it out slowly. "It was my fault."

"No, it wasn't."

His lips curved up in a humorless smile. "If I'd done the one thing she'd asked of me, Caro would be alive today."

"Your wife died because some drunk ran a traffic light, not because of forgotten cupcakes."

His gaze slid over her face, softened. "You're a good friend, Cassidy."

"The very best."

The lines of tension around his mouth eased at her impudent tone. He shook his head and chuckled. "What am I going to do with you?"

*Love me.* The words popped unbidden into her head and Cassidy could only be glad she hadn't spoken them aloud.

Time to put their relationship back where it belonged.

She slipped her hand downward and wrapped her fingers around the length of him. "I may have a suggestion or two."

As she'd hoped, desire erupted in his gaze, chasing away the shadows. "Again?"

In answer she rolled on top of him, watched his eyes darken as her breasts swung temptingly close to his mouth. She smiled down at him. "So, tell me, Doctor, are you up for a little game of 'Ride 'Em Cowboy'?"

## Chapter Nine

They made love three times that night. Tim didn't leave Cassidy's bed until nearly dawn. By the time he finally arrived home, all he wanted was a long nap.

But rest had to wait until he'd picked up his daughters. He'd barely hopped out of the shower and pulled on clean clothes to do just that when the hospital called. After notifying his parents, he was off and running.

By the time he got his patient stabilized, it was late afternoon.

"Lindsey told me you were out with that woman again." Suzanne jumped him the second he stepped into the foyer of his parents' home.

No need to ask who his mom meant, Tim thought.

Exhausted, the last thing Tim wanted to do was spar with his mother over Cassidy. He rubbed the bridge of his nose in an attempt to stop the headache threatening to form. "If you've spoken with Lindsey, then you know

Cassidy was already eating with them when I showed up to order a pizza."

Suzanne sniffed. "I think there is something suspicious about her being there at the same time as you."

Tim gave a humorless laugh. He was weary down to his very core. All he wanted was to pick up his daughters, go home and relax on the sofa while they played with their dolls. "Wow. Cass must be psychic, considering I only decided at the last minute to go there myself."

"Women like her have their ways," Suzanne insisted.

"Women like her?" Tim's tone turned cool but his mother didn't appear to notice.

"Out to snare themselves a doctor." His mother gave an exasperated huff as if she couldn't believe he was being so obtuse. "You'd be quite a coup. It's rare for a hairdresser to snag a rich physician husband."

"Cassidy and I are *friends*." He emphasized the word, met his mother's gaze squarely. "She's fun. I enjoy her company."

If his mom was flustered by his unwavering stare, it didn't show.

"She's not like Jayne." Suzanne nodded decisively as if that was a major point.

"I fail to see the relevance of that comment."

A soft mew at his feet had him looking down. Runt, er, Domino, fixed his golden eyes on Tim and mewed a second time. Heaving a resigned breath, he scooped the cat into his arms, where it began to purr.

His mother cast a disapproving glance at the cat before refocusing on her son. "Jayne would be a much better mother for the girls."

Tim scratched the cat behind the ears and once again failed to see the point. "I'm not looking for a wife or a mother for my children. We do just fine on our own."

"You're a good father," Suzanne acknowledged. "Your

dad and I are proud of how you've made your own way since Caro died. But surely you don't plan to be single forever."

Apparently done with being petted, Domino bit him. Tim jerked his hand back as the animal sprang and landed on the floor with a solid thud.

"I told your father we should get rid of him." His mother glared at the cat that had circled Tim's feet and now sat washing himself.

"He didn't break the skin—" Tim began but Suzanne waved him silent.

"You need a wife, Timothy. And my granddaughters need a mother."

"You know my schedule. It's obscene. How could I be a good husband to any woman?"

"Travis Fisher has a wife and five children," Suzanne pointed out.

"I'm not saying it can't be done." But as far as Tim was concerned, his partner was the exception to the rule. Travis never seemed stressed. The guy sailed through life with a smile on his lips. "I'm saying *I* can't do it. My focus needs to be Esther and Ellyn."

"Life can be lonely without a spouse at your side." Suzanne's voice softened. "I don't know what I'd do without your father."

"It can be lonely," Tim admitted. "Once the twins are in college, I'll reconsider."

"If you have to get your physical needs met, I suppose Cassidy Kaye would be appropriate." His mother's hand fluttered in the air. "Just be careful, son. Make sure there are no unwanted consequences."

Tim was stunned speechless. Had his mother really, with one careless remark and a dismissive wave, designated Cassidy—a smart, successful businesswoman—as a booty call?

"It's not like that between u—"

Esther and Ellyn rushed into the room and the moment was lost. But Tim vowed, the next time he had his mother alone, he was going to set her straight.


Cassidy tried to tell herself she hadn't really expected Tim to come when she'd invited him to the small open house celebrating five years in business. Still, as she gazed around the festively decorated salon, it felt as if everyone had someone. Everyone but her.

"You did this up right," her friend Hailey Ferris exclaimed, snagging a spring roll from a platter and popping it into her mouth.

"Congratulations." Hailey's husband, Winn, a successful business executive, leaned forward to brush a chaste kiss across her cheek.

"Thanks for coming." Cassidy knew both their schedules had been jam-packed today.

The two of them, newlyweds really, looked so happy together. Cassidy was thrilled Hailey, one of her best friends, had found a man who complemented her so fully.

*Tim and I are good together.* Cassidy shoved the thought aside. Wishing for something more than sex was a dead-end street.

"How is Tim?" Hailey asked slyly, gazing up at Cassidy through lowered lashes.

For a second Cassidy feared she'd spoken aloud. After all, up to this point Tim Duggan's name hadn't been mentioned. And why should it?

Cassidy feigned innocence. "Tim?"

Winn looked amused.

Hailey punched Cassidy's shoulder. "Don't play coy with me, missy. It doesn't suit you. I heard all about Friday night."

For just an instant, for one brief moment in time, Cassidy froze. Had someone seen Tim sneaking from her place in the early-morning hours? Was the news that he'd spent the night with her fueling the Jackson Hole gossip mill?

*What if it is?* Cassidy thought. *What if it is?* She and Tim were both consenting adults. They'd done nothing wrong. Although a few of their, ah, more adventurous moves might possibly be illegal in some states.

"Cat got your tongue?"

"That's a ridiculous expression." Cassidy softened the words with a smile. "My Friday involved running into Zach and Lindsey Taylor at Perfect Pizza. Tim stopped by the table and joined us for a few minutes."

Hailey's expression fell. "That's all?"

"The cream-cheese-and-pineapple special was de-lish," Cassidy told her.

"We'll have to check it out." Winn squeezed his wife's arm. "Cameron's practice will be over in ten minutes."

Cameron was Winn's son by a previous relationship. After the boy's mother died, Winn had received full custody.

"We'll do lunch next week and you can tell me all about the…pizza." Hailey gave Cassidy a quick hug. "Mega congrats on five years in business."

To Cassidy's surprise, Winn also hugged her. "You've got a great business here."

Coming from Winn, a man not known for saying nice things about other entrepreneurs, the compliment meant a lot.

They'd barely disappeared out the door when Cassidy heard a voice she hadn't expected to hear today.

"He's right, you know. You've grown this business from a one-woman shop to a Jackson Hole institution. All in five years."

Cassidy turned and saw Jayne Connors take a dainty sip of champagne. For a split second she wondered what the librarian was doing at her party. Until she remembered that Jayne was a customer.

"Thank you, Jayne."

While Cassidy wore black leggings, red heels and a psychedelic-print shirt that included every color *except* red and black, Jayne had draped a peach cashmere sweater over a sleeveless dove-gray linen dress.

Excruciatingly boring, but perfect for a doctor's wife.

A knife twisted in Cassidy's heart but she sidestepped the blood and forced a smile to her lips. "I'm happy you could make it."

Jayne took another sip from the plastic flute. "I wouldn't have missed it. This is a momentous occasion."

For one brief second Cassidy wondered if the librarian was being sarcastic, but a quick glance into her blue-green eyes reflected only sincerity.

"It takes a special person to start a business from scratch and build it," Jayne continued. "My mother has always wanted to open a small gift store. She says she hasn't done it yet because the time isn't right. That isn't the real reason."

Cassidy watched Jayne take another drink of champagne, a healthy one this time.

"What is the reason?" Cassidy asked when Jayne didn't elaborate.

"Fear."

The word hung in the air.

"I believe it's what keeps most of us from going after what we really want." Jayne's gaze met Cassidy's. "Don't you agree?"

Cassidy sensed there was a point to the question, though she wasn't sure what it could be. "I suppose."

"You know I'm right." Jayne took an open bottle of champagne from the table and refilled her empty glass.

"Unfortunately, I seem to have inherited the coward gene from my mother."

Jayne's tone was surprisingly melancholy and when the woman chugged half a glass of the bubbly in one gulp, Cassidy wondered how many glasses she'd already downed.

"I got the impression you enjoyed your position at the high school." In fact, Cassidy was sure of it. At the last task force meeting, Jayne had said she'd found her true calling in the education arena.

Surprise skittered across Jayne's face. "I love my job. There's nothing I'd rather do."

Now Cassidy was confused. "You said fear is keeping you from going after what you want."

"You know what I want." Jayne pointed a finger at her, chuckled.

Too much champagne. She was cutting Jayne off, Cassidy decided, her brow furrowing at the nonsensical reply. And making sure the librarian didn't drive home.

Cassidy smiled at Jayne. "I don't have a clue what you want."

"Not what I want." Jayne's gaze met Cassidy's. "*Who* I want."


Cassidy found herself thinking about that "who" several weeks later as she held the pregnancy test in her trembling hand.

Her period had always been regular. Until recently. Fear slithered up her spine, but she told herself—as she had for the past week—that this blip had to be due to stress. The Independence Day festivities had been obscene, business at the salon was ridiculous and her bridal business had spiked into the crazy range.

Despite the reassuring self-talk, the fingers holding the stick shook like an alcoholic with D.T.'s. *Stress*, she repeated to herself. *You're late because of stress.* What else could it be? While she wasn't on the pill, and she and Tim had used condoms each and every time.

She couldn't be pregnant.

She simply couldn't be pregnant.

When she began to feel light-headed from her heart slamming against her rib cage, Cassidy made herself look at the stick she held. Then she glanced at the box propped up on the vanity counter for easy reference.

Positive.

Tears filled her eyes. Fighting the nausea rising like a tsunami inside her, Cassidy jerked to her feet.

She would go for a run. She would eat a pint of cookie-dough ice cream. She would *deal*.

All her life she'd handled whatever curveballs the often unkind world had thrown at her. Granted, this was a bit more of a challenge than having the wrong salon chair delivered two times in a row, but nothing she couldn't handle.

As she slipped out the door and headed down the steps, Cassidy reassured herself she would handle this catastrophe.

She only wished she knew how…

Sitting in the quiet of the doctors' lounge, Tim sipped his coffee and stared at his phone. He was surprised to see the text from Cassidy. In the weeks since he'd spent the night, she hadn't contacted him. Not once.

Neither had he contacted her. He'd wanted to see her again. He couldn't remember the last time he'd enjoyed himself so much. And while the sex had been off the charts, it had been merely the cherry atop a totally enjoyable evening.

Not since before Caro died had Tim shared his deepest thoughts and feelings with another human being. When he'd left Cassidy's place that morning, he'd had every intention of calling her again. Not because of the sex—okay, that was definitely part of it—but also because of their deepening friendship.

His conversation with his mother, though, had unintended consequences. Cassidy wasn't a booty call. Yet, wasn't sleeping with her when he had no intention of pursuing a relationship treating her like she was one?

Not that Cassidy had given any indication she expected more. But she deserved better.

Tim stared at his phone. Reread the message.

We need to talk. Tonight. Five p.m. Elk Refuge.

"Problem?"

Tim jerked his attention from the phone.

Travis stared quizzically, a jelly donut in one hand, a cup of coffee in the other. He gestured to Tim's phone with the hand holding the donut. "Something wrong?"

"Not at all." Tim forced an easy smile, but during the short conversation with his partner, his mind kept returning to the text.

Perhaps Cassidy contacting him wasn't so odd, but the meeting location was definitely strange.

The Elk Refuge sat on the edge of the city of Jackson. There were walking paths, popular with both locals and tourists, but at five the place would likely be deserted. Which seemed to indicate Cassidy wanted privacy.

Try as he might, Tim couldn't figure out what this was all about. Well, there was only one way to find out.

Once Travis left, Tim pulled out his phone.

It's a date, he keyed in and pressed Send.

## *Chapter Ten*

Tim saw Cassidy the second he pulled into the lot. Dressed in jeans, a silver shirt that shimmered in the sunlight and bright red boots, she stood at the entrance to the refuge. He wondered if it was the jet-black hair or the glare of the sun that made her look so pale.

He parked next to her car in the empty lot. As he strode across the gravel, stones crunched beneath his leather loafers, imparting a fine sheen of dust. He felt overdressed in his dark gray dress pants and pin-striped button down, but he'd come straight from the clinic.

"Hey, stranger. It's good to see you," he said, keeping it light when he drew close, resisting the urge to pull her into his arms and kiss her.

The truth was he'd missed her. A lot. Keeping his distance had proved more difficult than he'd imagined. But it had been necessary. He wasn't looking to fall in love again or to marry, and Cassidy deserved all that and more.

While the cheeky smile she shot him was familiar,

there were dark circles beneath her eyes that even makeup couldn't disguise. Her eyes, normally bright and filled with sass, looked red rimmed and haunted.

"I realize it was short notice and a hassle, especially with the girls…" She stopped, pressing her bright red lips together as if realizing she was babbling.

"No worries." He kept his tone conversational, his smile reassuring despite the concern bubbling up inside him.

Something was wrong. At work? With her…family? Tim vowed he would find out and do whatever he could to help. He was thankful she felt comfortable coming to him for assistance.

"Well, I appreciate your willingness to meet me." She blinked rapidly as if trying to dislodge a speck of dust from her eyes.

The next he knew she'd spun on the heels of her boots. She started down the path that wound through the refuge at such a fast clip it took Tim several long strides to catch up to her.

Even when he reached her, she kept her gaze focused on a herd of buffalo in the far distance. Lines of tension bracketed her mouth and eyes. Whatever was troubling her was obviously serious.

They strode down the dusty path surrounded by rangeland in silence.

Finally, Tim could no longer stand the suspense. Until he knew the problem, he couldn't help, couldn't reassure her that all would be well. He reached over, took her arm, slowing her pace until she stopped.

"Tell me what's wrong," he ordered in a tone that brooked no argument.

"As if you care."

The scorn-filled words appeared to startle her as much as him.

"I'm sorry." She raked a shaky hand through the shiny black hair. "It's not fair to take this out on you."

"I care about you. That's why I'm here. I want to help. Tell me how." He placed his hands on her arms and searched those large, expressive eyes. The depth of fear and uncertainty reflected there surprised him. "Are you in some sort of trouble, Cass?"

"You could say that." She took a deep breath and squared her shoulders. "I'm pregnant."

His hands dropped to his sides and, without realizing what he was doing, he took a step back.

"It's your kid." She lifted her chin in a defiant tilt. "I know we used condoms but I haven't been with anyone else in…in years."

Tim's brilliant mind, the one that had propelled him to the top of his medical school class, dissolved into a pile of mush. He tried to form a coherent thought, but only one circled in his brain. Pregnant. Cassidy was pregnant. With his child.

"Are…are you sure?" he finally managed to sputter.

"I took a pregnancy test." She gave a little laugh, then her voice hitched. "Actually, I've taken three. All were positive."

Tim rubbed the bridge of his nose and fought for a voice that did not shake. "Have you seen a doctor?"

She shook her head and her gaze returned to the buffalo. "I prefer no one know."

"They'll find out eventually."

"Perhaps."

A cold knot formed in the pit of his stomach.

A step at a time, he reminded himself. "We can't discuss options, ah, future plans, until we confirm the pregnancy."

She nodded. "I've thought about seeing a doctor in Idaho Falls."

That was one solution. However, it would likely take several weeks to get an appointment. Tim wanted answers now.

Though it wasn't ideal, he had a more immediate solution. "We could go back to my office."

Before she could respond, Tim pulled his phone from his pocket and checked the time. "Everyone should have left by now. I could do a quick check. We'd know for sure tonight."

It had been an impulsive offer. Tim half expected her to protest. Instead her lips quirked upward.

"Kind of kinky, Duggan."

"Not kinky." Tim spoke quickly. "I'm a professional and—"

"Yeah, yeah." A devilish gleam had replaced the fear in Cassidy's blue eyes. "Do the check. I mean, it isn't like you haven't seen me naked."

Tim laughed. As they strolled back to their vehicles, he took her hand, reassured when she didn't pull away.

Yet, as he drove to his office with Cassidy's car in his rearview mirror, Tim had the sinking feeling life as he knew it was about to change.

After the baby check was over, Cassidy suggested a walk, her thoughts racing like a sports car at full throttle. She needed to move, *had* to move.

She had no idea what Tim was thinking. He'd been totally professional, taking her menstrual history, doing the exam with great care and sensitivity.

When he'd finished, the bleak look in his eyes told her all she needed to know. The three positive tests hadn't lied. She was indeed pregnant.

*A baby.*

Cassidy didn't know the first thing about babies. She liked kids, sure. But to care for one, to be the one responsible for raising that child, well, that scared the heck out of her.

They entered the residential area just south of his office building, an area of green lawns and leafy trees. An area teeming with kids.

Kids on bikes.

Kids shooting baskets in the driveway.

Kids playing on porches.

Cassidy closed her eyes momentarily and shuddered.

"What are you thinking?" Tim's tone was soft, inviting conversation.

"I'm thinking this sucks. Big-time."

Tim nodded. A muscle jumped in his jaw. "I'll second that assessment."

"We used protection." Her voice rose and anger flashed in her blue eyes. "Even in the shower."

"We did." Tim also recalled that, when he'd been tempted to skip the condom in the shower, Cassidy had insisted.

"No method of birth control, save abstinence, is one hundred percent effective," he said woodenly. The response he'd given a thousand times was now all too relevant.

Cassidy gave a humorless laugh. "I can't hit the lottery but this long shot comes in to bite me in the ass."

"To bite *us* in the ass," Tim clarified. "We're in this together, Cass."

While Tim understood he had little say in her decision about how to handle this pregnancy, she needed to understand he wouldn't abandon her.

She studied him, her expression blank, giving nothing away. "It's my body."

Though his heart slammed against his rib cage, Tim managed a nonchalant tone. "What does that mean?"

"It means that now that I know this is really happening, I have a lot to consider. I need to—"

Before she could say more, he held up a hand. "I meant it when I said we're in this together. For now, and for the long haul. You can count on me. I'll be there for you and our child." He swallowed hard. "It might be a good idea for us to get married."

He'd taken her by surprise, he could see that by the way her eyes flew open wide, in the moment of stunned silence.

"Marriage?" Her hand fluttered in the air. "You don't love me."

*Love? Who said anything about love?* But something in her eyes, in the vulnerable look on her face had Tim choosing his words carefully. "I like you, Cassidy. I like you a lot. And we're going to have a baby."

"Maybe."

The words, spoken so casually, stole his breath. "What are you saying?"

For a second she looked puzzled. Then her eyes softened. "I simply meant that lots of women have miscarriages during the first part of their pregnancy. Right?"

Tim exhaled a breath he didn't realize he'd been holding. "That sometimes happens."

"I don't think we need to rush into any kind of decisions," she said. "What's the break point?"

"Break point?"

She smiled at his obviously baffled expression. Her first genuine smile since the bomb had dropped. "When is there less of a chance of miscarriage?"

"After the first trimester the risk drops significantly."

Cassidy nodded. "Then we'll keep this pregnancy our little secret for now."

He shoved his hands into his pockets, kept his tone casual. "You plan to continue it, the pregnancy, I mean."

"I'll continue. But I don't know if I'll keep it. The kid, I mean."

Tim froze. While adoption was certainly a viable alternative, all Tim could think was this was *his* baby she was considering giving up.

*A step at a time*, he reminded himself. "You need to start prenatal care."

Cassidy paused then gazed up at him through lowered lashes. "I realize this might be asking a lot, but will you be my doctor?"


The next few weeks Cassidy barely had time to think. She'd made it clear when they'd confirmed the pregnancy she needed time to process and she'd contact Tim when she was ready to talk further. She'd warned him that might not be until the next month when it was time for her first after-hours appointment.

Summer was crazy busy with weddings booked most weekends. She didn't have time to be pregnant. Or to think about all the ways this might impact her life.

Every day, Cassidy tried not to think of the baby growing inside her. That had proven more difficult than she'd anticipated. Especially at first, when her breasts ached and she was exhausted all the time.

Thankfully, while fried foods tended to make her stomach churn, she hadn't experienced much nausea. In fact, if it wasn't for the fatigue, she'd never have felt better.

After banishing all junk food—including Oreos—from her apartment, Cassidy had given the rest of the beer in her fridge to a client. She'd taken up drinking water. Never missed a vitamin. Faithfully exercised.

Cassidy couldn't recall ever being so healthy. This baby might have been a surprise and might not even take but she was doing her best to keep him—or her—healthy and safe.

Initially, Tim respected her request to keep his distance. Then, several weeks ago, he'd begun texting her. Every day. Little notes about what he was doing and how his day had gone. Sometimes he shared funny anecdotes about the girls.

She saw no harm in responding. The texts they exchanged quickly became something she looked forward to each day. Then, several days ago, he'd invited her to a barbecue at his parents' home.

Thx. Sorry. Can't.

Cassidy's finger had been poised above the send button when she'd hesitated.

Would it be so wrong to accept? She wanted to see Tim. Texting just wasn't the same. Last week, when they sat in that room listening to their baby's heartbeat and he'd taken her hand, her heart had melted.

He'd made it clear how much he'd like it if she could get to know his daughters better. After all, the baby would be the twins' half sibling. Neither of them brought up the fact she hadn't made any decisions about their child.

But a *family* barbecue. At of all places, his parents' home.

Cassidy had run across Tim's mother recently at a fundraiser for the library. The woman had been surprisingly cordial.

There was, of course, a simple explanation for Suzanne Duggan's sunny mood. In the past month, there had been zero sightings of Cassidy with her son.

Her lips curved in a smile. Cassidy deleted the message she'd been about to send and keyed in a different reply.

The sound of the whoosh told her the acceptance was on its way. Cassidy only wished she could be a fly on the wall when Tim told his mother who he was bringing to dinner.

Tim was furious. Not simply angry. Not a little upset. *Furious.*

He clenched his hands into fists at his sides and glared at his mother. Because of the proximity to the unexpected guests in his parents' backyard, Tim spoke in a terse whisper. "You told me this was a *family* dinner."

"It is." Though her expression had turned wary, her tone was light and breezy. "Your father is here. Lindsey and Zach are manning the grill. And you and the girls are here."

"As are the Connorses." Tim fought to control the anger rising inside him. He'd finally gotten Cassidy to accept one of his invitations and now his mother pulled this stunt? "When did they become family?"

"I don't understand why you're upset. Cassidy Kaye isn't part of this family, yet you invited her." His mother turned accusing eyes in his direction. "You didn't even ask me. Just announced she was coming."

"With *me*," Tim emphasized, holding on to his temper with both hands. "I told you she was coming as my guest."

"Well, the Connorses are here as *my* guests." Suzanne's tight smile was unapologetic. "Besides, I think having Jayne here will be a good thing."

"How do you figure that?"

"You'll see Jayne and Cassidy together." His mother's tone was blissfully confident. "Jayne will shine by comparison."

"Don't be so certain."

His mother's perfectly arched brows pulled together in a frown. "I thought whatever was between you and that woman was done. You haven't spoken of her in weeks, haven't so much as mentioned her name."

"We've both had difficulty finding free time." It wasn't entirely the truth. Yes, Cass had been busy. But the fact was, she hadn't wanted to see him. A surprising kick to the gut. "The task force and the salon have been keeping her busy."

Suzanne set the bowl of potato salad on the table with precise movement, her jaw set in a hard angle. "You're telling me it's not over between the two of you."

"Not by a long shot."

Out of the corner of his eye, Tim saw Cassidy step through the open gate leading to his parents' backyard. He smiled. She reminded him of a brilliant Amazon parrot trying to go incognito as a brown wren.

Her hair hung to her shoulders in loose curls, the strands a pretty golden blond. Not a single streak of blue or pink anywhere. Her clothes were also startlingly demure. Instead of the bright, flashy styles she normally wore, she had on jeans and a blue shirt. Granted, the shirt was a bright royal blue but it was still a simple cotton tee.

He found her magnificent.

"Behave yourself," Tim warned his mother and hurried across the yard, eager to greet his guest.

## Chapter Eleven

Though her smile never wavered, Cassidy froze when she saw Jayne Connors standing beside Suzanne Duggan. When Tim had said this was a family backyard barbecue, she'd expected, well, she'd assumed only family would be here.

Cassidy had spent much of her childhood feeling as if she was on the outside looking in, so this unease was nothing new. But the disappointment that surged strong and fast took her by surprise.

She hadn't planned to come at all. While she had to admit it was nice seeing Tim, just because she was pregnant with his baby didn't mean they had to hang out. Other than, of course, when necessary.

Like last week when she'd slipped into Tim's office late one night for a brief encounter of the medical kind. When the strong, fast heartbeat of the baby—*their* child—had filled the room, she hadn't been able to keep the goofy grin from her lips. She might have been embarrassed if the same grin hadn't lifted Tim's mouth, as well...

"I'm glad you came. For a second I thought you might have changed your mind."

Cassidy shifted and saw a hint of uncertainty in the familiar hazel eyes. Instead of taking a step forward—which was a completely ridiculous impulse—she simply smiled.

"Thanks for the invite." Pulling her gaze from Tim, Cassidy glanced around the large fenced backyard.

Her eyes were immediately drawn to the gorgeous patio. Edged with flowers that were either fake or on steroids, she noted the plants were placed strategically for maximum visual impact. Despite all the weddings Cassidy had attended, she had no idea what kind of flowers they were or which one of the colorful varieties was emitting such an enticing fragrance.

As amazing as the flowers were, it was the grill station that captured her gaze and held it. Under a pergola of redwood, the massive steel-fronted grill was encased in stone and brick. The countertop had more space than the one in her apartment. Of course, she'd venture the Duggans did more cooking here during nice weather than Cassidy did in her kitchen all year.

There was only one negative. The grill with its dozens of shiny silver knobs released a nauseating aroma of sizzling meat into the air.

Not certain if it was nerves or brats, Cassidy ignored the churning and watched Zach turn the meat tongs over to his father-in-law then give his wife's hand a squeeze.

Even from this distance, Lindsey looked a little green. Perhaps the brats had gotten to her, too. If Cassidy hadn't known Tim's sister was pregnant, she'd never have guessed. Lindsey's navy cropped pants hugged a slender figure without even the tiniest bulge.

Of course, this was early days for her, just like it was

for Cassidy. For a brief second, Cassidy had an image of her child and Lindsey's little one playing together in this yard under the shade of the large oak tree.

She immediately banished the image as premature. Cassidy still hadn't decided what to do once the baby was born. Though she told herself she'd do what was best for the child, the thought of giving up a part of her—a part of Tim—to strangers tore at her like a rusty nail on smooth flesh.

But that was future stuff. First she had to get past the crucial twelve-week mark. Her hand moved protectively to her flat stomach.

Tim cleared his throat.

Cassidy reined in her thoughts and gestured to the two men next to the grill. "Your dad and Emerson look like they're having fun."

Tim's father held meat tongs in a classic fencing pose, while Emerson swiped at them with a two-prong fork. The two only laughed when Suzanne called out for them to act their age.

"About Emerson being here—"

"He's your dad's friend. It's fine. I thought you said it'd be just family but—" Cassidy paused, horrified. Dear Lord, were those tears filling her eyes? *Darn pregnancy hormones.*

She blinked the moisture back before Tim could notice and waved a hand. "The more the merrier."

"My parents invited them. I didn't know they were coming myself until I got here." Tim's arm draped around her shoulders and he leaned close, his gaze intense. "We don't have to stay."

*Get a grip.* Cassidy gave herself a swift mental kick. As much as she'd like his arm to stay just where it was, it was a little too…intimate. She lifted a shoulder and took a step back, dislodging the connection.

"We're not going anywhere. At least I'm not. I came here specifically to get a taste of Lindsey's corn salad. We were talking at Perfect Pizza before you got there that night. She mentioned it was a favorite of the girls'. When she said there were Fritos on top, I knew I had to try it." Cassidy stopped the chatter and took a breath. "Besides, this is the perfect opportunity for Jayne and me to chat about something of personal interest to us both."

Tim's brows pulled together in puzzlement. "What would that be?"

Cassidy winked. "Why, you, of course."

A startled look flashed across Tim's face, but before he had a chance to respond, his father called out and motioned them over.

With each step, the odor, er, aroma, from the smokin' hot monster grew more intense. Bile rose in Cassidy's throat. She fought it by breathing through her mouth.

Both men greeted her and Tim with friendly smiles.

"Hello, Miss Cassidy." Tim's dad lifted his tongs in greeting. "I'm glad you could join us today."

"Good to see you again, pretty lady," Emerson added, his meat fork no longer at a dueling level.

As they chatted, Tim's hand rested proprietarily on the small of her back. When warmth flooded her body, Cassidy scolded herself for responding to such a simple gesture.

They'd barely made it through a few comments about the beautiful weather when Jayne wandered over. Cassidy wasn't surprised to see the librarian had eschewed jeans for a pencil-thin navy skirt and a crisp white shirt. A scarf with a nautical flair was looped artistically around her throat.

Cassidy thought of the tulle skirt and the tie-dyed tank she'd considered wearing today and wished she'd worn the ensemble. Though she hadn't wanted to stand out, she realized her everyday clothes gave her confidence.

Wearing what she wanted, doing as she pleased, re-affirmed to her that she was no longer a scared little girl subject to her mother's crazy mood swings. She was a woman in charge of her own destiny. Today, she needed that confidence.

As she visited with Jayne, Cassidy was seized with an uncharacteristic urge to take Tim's hand. Why, she wasn't certain. To show Jayne she was here with him? To say they were connected in a way not yet obvious?

Cassidy kept her hands at her sides.

She didn't need anyone. The only person she'd ever been able to count on was herself. This needy uncertainty was new and extremely annoying.

*It's just the hormones*, she reassured herself. Or perhaps it was this whole crazy wholesome scene. A backyard bar-becue on a Friday night. With a normal family. Excluding Suzanne, of course.

Still, at least she didn't have to worry about Tim's mother snorting cocaine at the table or screaming obscenities at the top of her lungs over nothing. That was the kind of home life she'd had as a child.

Though Tim kept a respectable distance, Cassidy found his presence beside her comforting. For some reason, she'd expected him to remove his palm from her back once Jayne draw near, but it remained firmly against her spine. Cassidy felt the heat all the way through the fabric of her shirt.

"How's the task force coming?" Tim asked, bringing up a subject they could all discuss.

Before she or Jayne could respond, the twins ran up, talking a mile a minute.

Jayne smiled indulgently. "Slow down. I can't under-stand a word either of you are saying."

Tim laughed. "That makes two of us."

"They found a frog and want us to come see it." A fast

talker herself, Cassidy had no difficulty interpreting the high-pitched, jumbled-together words. "A huge green one."

"He's by the fence. Ellyn is scared." Esther's tone made it clear what she thought of her sister's fear. "Come see."

"You go on." Jayne wrinkled her nose. "I'm not a fan of anything slimy."

Cassidy glanced around the fenced yard. Not a pond in sight. Not even a small decorative one. "They normally like water."

Jayne shuddered. "Just get rid of it."

"Noooo," Esther protested.

"Let's take a look." Without thinking, Cassidy extended a hand.

Esther took it readily, pulling her across the lawn.

While Jayne remained behind, Tim and Ellyn followed.

Esther tugged Cassidy all the way to the far corner of the yard, where decorative bushes in vibrant colors of red, gold and green had been expertly trimmed.

The amphibian sat big and bold in front of a gold-leafed bush.

"He is a big boy." Cassidy squatted down to get a closer look. The large green frog stared back. "And quite a beauty."

Ellyn spoke up from somewhere behind her.

"He's…slimy," she said in a hesitant tone, her words echoing Jayne's opinion.

"Good observation." Cassidy glanced over her shoulder and smiled. "The sheen helps his skin stay moist when he's not in water."

She turned back to the frog and Esther squatted down beside her. Cassidy motioned with her hand for Ellyn to also move closer. "Girls, look at how pretty he is with his shiny green skin. And don't you just love his black polka dots?"

Okay, so the dark spots weren't really polka dots, but what good was an imagination if you didn't use it?

"I bet he's a she," Esther announced. "Boys don't wear polka dots, do they, Daddy?"

Behind her, Cassidy heard Tim chuckle. "Not usually."

"I have a polka-dot dress," Esther told Cassidy quite seriously. "But my dots are pink."

Though Ellyn still appeared hesitant, she edged closer until she stood beside Cassidy, digging the toe of one shoe into the dirt.

"His eyes are bulgy," Ellyn observed.

"They stick up like that so he can see in several directions at the same time." Cassidy kept her tone matter-of-fact. "He's curious. Just like you girls. Curiosity is a good thing."

Cassidy glanced back and caught Tim staring, a look of approval in his warm hazel eyes.

"Jenna in our class at school has bulgy eyes," Ellyn announced.

Tim covered his laughter with a cough.

"But she doesn't have green skin," Esther told her twin then refocused on Cassidy, her intense gaze reminding Cassidy of Tim. "I like bright colors."

Cassidy grinned. "You and me both, chickadee."

"I like it when you have those pretty colors in your hair," Ellyn surprised Cassidy by saying.

"I do, too," Tim agreed.

Cassidy straightened, angled her head. "You do?"

All three nodded.

"Though you look very nice today," Tim quickly added. As if he could hear her unspoken thoughts, he smiled. "I believe what my daughters and me are saying is that we like you however you wear your hair."

The weight that had been pulling her heart into the basement began to lift.

"What are you doing back here?" Suzanne scolded as she moved cautiously through the grass, looking perfectly groomed—as usual—in khaki pants and red-checkered shirt.

"Gramma." Ellyn hopped and ran to her grandmother tugging on her hand. "Come see the pretty frog."

"Don't touch it." Suzanne pulled her granddaughter close. "You get warts from those things."

"Mom." Tim looked mildly amused. "Warts are caused by a human virus, not by touching frogs or toads."

"So *you* say," Suzanne said dismissively, tightly clutching her granddaughter's hand. "There's a stick over there. Kill it."

The cry of the girls nearly drowned out her words.

"Nooooo," Esther cried.

"Don't kill it," Ellyn said, tears filling her eyes.

Tim cast his mother a censuring glance. "No one is killing anything."

"Of course not." Cassidy spoke in a reassuring manner. "But your grandmother is right. He doesn't belong in this yard."

The two girls focused on her even as Cassidy shifted her gaze to Suzanne and spoke directly to her. "Do you happen to have an empty shoebox?"

Suzanne's brows pulled together in puzzlement. "Why?"

"It's time we take Mr. Frog to a new home."

Tim insisted on driving Cassidy home after the barbecue. The girls were playing happily with Miss Priss and her bad-boy baby, Domino. They happily waved goodbye when he told them he'd be back shortly. His father had given Cassidy a warm hug and told her he was glad she'd come and to not be such a stranger.

Even his mother had been cordial. At least what passed for cordial for Suzanne Duggan. She'd thanked Cassidy for ridding her yard of the green menace and even managed to sound sincere. In deference to her, Tim waited until they were out of sight before capturing Cassidy's hand.

"What's this?" Cassidy lifted their joined hands.

Tim pretended to study their fingers, his straight-cut nails and her purple-tipped ones. "It's me touching you, something I wanted to do all evening."

She didn't smile or shoot back some pithy remark guaranteed to make him grin. Instead, she pulled her hand from his.

"You don't have to do this, you know," she said softly, her expression serious.

"Do what? Be nice?"

"Pretend to be interested in me." Cassidy stopped at the edge of the driveway and faced him. "While I appreciate it, we both know you're only hanging with me now because of the bun."

Tim cocked his head. Sometimes it was as if she spoke a foreign language.

"In the oven." Cassidy patted her flat belly.

He almost grinned but pulled the smile back at the last second.

Her blue eyes were so serious and there was an uncharacteristic frown between her brows. He also saw fatigue and weariness in the way her shoulders, normally so straight, drooped.

He raised his hand and cupped her cheek. "I'm with you because I like you."

She shook her head. "You made it clear, BB—Before Bun—that you didn't have time for a relationship."

Instead of answering, he glanced from the driveway to the street. "Where's your car?"

"Down the block. With your parents living on a circle, I wasn't sure where to park." Her gaze met his. "You don't need to drive me."

"You're not driving home alone at night."

A startled look crossed her face. "It's not even dark."

"If I have to ride in the trunk, I'm coming with you."

"In the trunk, huh?" She tapped a nail against her lips. "That might be interesting."

He just grinned and when she started down the sidewalk toward her vehicle, Tim fell into step beside her.

"I had the next ten years of my life planned out," Tim said finally, turning serious. "Then you showed up."

Her chuckle sounded forced. "And turned your life upside down."

Tim opened her car door. He didn't dispute it. How could he? It was true. But an upside-down life wasn't a bad thing, or so he kept telling himself.

"I want to get to know you, Cassidy." He slanted a sideways glance and was once again reminded how different she looked this evening. "The real you."

"I'm always me."

"Not dressed like that."

Her lips twitched. "You don't like boring?"

"You'd be beautiful in a burlap sack." He reached over and took her hand. "You don't need to change your hair or clothes to prove you belong."

"Is that what you think I was trying to do?" Her voice had turned cool.

"Weren't you?" That was one of the things he liked most about Cassidy. They could be honest with each other.

She hesitated for a long moment. "I wanted to fit in."

"Not possible." At her startled look, he grinned. "You're unique. One of a kind. Don't change, Cass. Not for me. Not for anyone."

The drive to her downtown apartment went by all too quickly. He parked and they stopped outside the door that would take her up the steps to her second-story apartment.

"Will you invite me up?"

She hesitated then shook her head. "It's been a long day."

His gaze searched hers. "I want us to start dating. I want you to get to know my girls and let them get to know you."

"Because of the baby."

"Partly. The baby will be their sibling," Tim said finally. "You and I will forever be joined by our child."

Cassidy gave a humorless laugh and pretended to shiver. "Now that's one scary thought."

He found himself encouraged that she didn't mention the possibility of not keeping the baby.

"Seriously, Cass. I think it's important we use this time before our child is born to get to know each other better."

"I'd say we know each other pretty...intimately."

If she thought the suggestive tone and wiggling eyebrows would distract him, it only proved how little she knew him.

"What do you say?" Tim pressed. "Will you go out with me tomorrow night?"

## Chapter Twelve

Cassidy still wasn't quite sure how it happened, but she was dating Tim Duggan.

Of course, she knew how it had happened, she corrected her thoughts. She'd gotten herself knocked up. He was being a gentleman.

The real question was, how had she ended up shopping for baby stuff with his sister?

"What do you think of this?" Lindsey held up a one-piece garment that looked incredibly tiny with little snaps and a picture of a red dump truck on the front.

"It looks like it's made for a doll." Cassidy fought a frisson of fear. Would her baby really be so small?

Lindsey examined the tag. "It says zero to three months, so it should fit a newborn."

Tim's sister had stopped into the salon at the end of Cassidy's workday. The women had headed to Babies R Us, a boutique not far from the hair salon. After standing on her feet all day, shopping didn't interest her but Lindsey had sounded so hopeful when she'd asked if Cassidy had plans. If she was going to make an effort to become better acquainted with Tim's family, spending time with Lindsey—a woman she liked—seemed a good place to start.

Cassidy glanced at the garment, not even tempted to pick it up. "I'm surprised you didn't ask your mother to shop with you."

Lindsey gave a little laugh. "And have her lecture me on how much weight I'm gaining, or not gaining? No, thank you."

Cassidy looked at her askance. "I thought the two of you were getting along better?"

At the barbecue two weeks ago, Cassidy hadn't heard Suzanne direct a single snide comment at her daughter. Lindsey put down the garment and picked up another one. Only this one, instead of having a truck on the front, had a pink princess. "It's up and down. Mom can be a tad overbearing. In case you hadn't noticed."

"I noticed," Cassidy said with a wry smile.

"Tim pretty much ignores her." Lindsey moved on to more little outfits hanging on impossibly small hangers on a circular rack. "That's always worked for him. Our sister, Sarah, could do no wrong. She and Mom got along wonderfully. But her and me…"

A look of sadness filled Lindsey's eyes. Then she fixed those eyes, so much like her brother's, on Cassidy. "What about you? How do you and your mom get along?"

"We haven't spoken in years." Cassidy kept her tone light. "Unless you count all the times she's called to ask for money to bail her out of jail."

Lindsey winced. "Ouch."

"I used to give it to her," Cassidy admitted. "But I made it clear the last time that the well has dried up."

"Were you two close…when you were growing up?"

Cassidy wished she'd never gone shopping with Lindsey. Her other friends, Hailey and Daffodil, knew the topic of her mother and her less-than-happy childhood were off-limits. But Lindsey didn't have a clue. She was simply making conversation as they attempted to get to know each other better.

"Never." Cassidy kept all emotion from her voice. "If you look up *bad mother* in the dictionary, her picture would be front and center."

Lindsey giggled then clapped a hand over her mouth. "I'm sorry. I was just thinking you'd find my mom's picture under *bossy mother*."

Cassidy couldn't help but smile. There was really so much to like about Lindsey.

"What I hate about having such a mother is that I have no compass." Cassidy picked up an infant dress in bright pink and purple, the fabric as soft as a caress. She resisted a sudden urge to rub it against her cheek. "I have no clue if I'll be a good mother. The thought of being a parent, being responsible for an innocent little human being, scares me to death."

The fingers holding the dress began to tremble. Cassidy knew how to take care of herself, how to protect herself. But taking care of someone else, especially one so small, had a knot forming in the pit of her stomach. Babies didn't come with road maps. What if she kept the child only to screw it up?

"That's why it's good when there are two parents in the home." Lindsey shot her a pointed glance. "Tim is a great dad."

Something in Lindsey's eyes had Cassidy putting the dress back on the rack and feigning nonchalance. "He is a good dad to the girls."

"And he'll be a good dad to your baby." Lindsey's tone was matter-of-fact as she turned to a display of cloth diapers.

It took a second for the woman's words to penetrate. Cassidy moved to her side. "What did you say?"

"You heard me." Lindsey waved a dismissive hand. "Don't deny it. The signs are all there."

Of course, Cassidy thought with a little bitterness, the way Tim had been hovering around her the past few weeks. What other reason could there be for his sudden interest in her?

"Only pregnant women frequent the john as much as you and me." Lindsey's lips twisted in a wry smile. "And I saw you yawning the other night at the Lassiters' party. It was barely eight o'clock."

Horror rippled through Cassidy. She hadn't realized she'd been so obvious. If Lindsey had noticed, someone else may have made the connection, as well. "Who else knows?"

"No one," Lindsey set down the diaper. "I haven't even mentioned my suspicions to Zach. Or Tim."

"What secrets are you holding back from me, little sister?"

The masculine voice from behind had the two women jumping.

"It's not me who has secrets, dear brother." Lindsey lifted a brow. "Have you told Mom she's going to be a grandmother again?"

Tim's smile disappeared. His gaze shifted from his sister to Cassidy then back to his sister. "I was there the other night when you told her you and Zach were pregnant. Remember?"

"I'm not talking about me and Zach." Her gaze slanted to Cassidy, who stood frozen in place.

Cassidy looked from Lindsey to Tim. She realized Tim must have been who Lindsey had texted earlier. How else would he have known where to find them?

"I want to know why I had to guess." Lindsey pointed

a finger at her brother. "Why didn't you tell me you were going to be a daddy again?"

Cassidy pulled herself from her stupor. "Just like you and Zach, we wanted to wait until after the first trimester."

"Okay, okay, I get it." A look of understanding filled Lindsey's eyes. "Zach and I celebrated with sparkling grape juice when I hit twelve weeks."

"It won't be long before I hit that mark," Cassidy heard herself admit.

"Then it'll be your and Tim's turn to celebrate."

Cassidy shook her head. "I hardly think an unplanned pregnancy is a cause for celebration."

Lindsey squeezed her hand. "Welcoming a new life into the world is always a reason to celebrate."

"I just realized," Tim said, "that our babies will be born close to the same time. They'll grow up together."

"That will be so cool." Lindsey smiled at Cassidy.

To Cassidy, it all sounded so…so normal. But she didn't do normal. Didn't know what normal looked like. And, regardless of Lindsey's reassuring words, she wasn't confident she was wired for motherhood.

She considered mentioning that she might give the child up for adoption, but knew that would only prolong this conversation.

"I thought you were delivering a baby," Cassidy asked Tim, desperate to change the subject. "At least that's what Lindsey said."

"This one just popped out." Tim appeared oblivious to the edge in her tone. "If only all deliveries could be so quick and easy."

Cassidy didn't expect him to call regularly or keep her informed of his day-to-day activities. The fact that she hadn't heard from him in several days was perfectly fine with her.

For her, it had been business as usual. She'd worked in

the salon, had a task force meeting and last evening attended a fund-raiser at the Spring Gulch Country Club.

The fact that she'd kept glancing around the ballroom for a certain someone made her angry. The highlight of the evening was when she ran into Keenan McGregor, a friend from the old neighborhood. He'd been there with his wife, Mitzi, a prominent orthopedic surgeon in Jackson Hole.

Keenan had been alone when she bumped into him and they'd spent a considerable amount of time talking. When he'd mentioned he'd heard she'd been dating Tim, she'd found herself spilling her guts to the man she loved like a brother.

He'd listened as she explained all the reasons she wasn't mother material. Then he'd hugged her tight and told her he believed she could be whatever she set her mind to be.

Cassidy wanted to believe him. Up to this point, she'd always trusted Keenan's judgment. But this situation was different. The stakes were so much higher...

When Tim asked Cassidy to spend Sunday with him and the girls, she hesitated. She didn't want him to think he could just snap his fingers and she'd be available. But she'd always been a realist. When the pregnancy could no longer be hidden and it came out that Tim was the father, there would be lots of talk.

He was a prominent physician in Jackson Hole. She was a successful businesswoman.

If they were regularly seen together prior to the pregnancy news hitting the gossip mill, it would look as if they'd had some sort of relationship, which would go a long way toward quieting the talk. Not that Cassidy cared about wagging tongues, but she didn't want the baby or the twins or Tim to be hurt by careless gossip.

She glanced at the clock on the wall. Three in the afternoon. Hardly the whole day, but Tim and the girls had attended Sunday services then had lunch at his parents'. She'd been invited, but had declined.

Glancing down, Cassidy inspected her appearance. The lime-green biker shorts and black graphic tee seemed appropriate for an afternoon bike ride at Yellowstone.

The love of outdoor activities was one thing she and Tim had in common. Since she loved heels and clothes, she knew he'd been surprised by her love of biking, hiking and everything outdoors.

Physical activity had always been a good stress reliever for her. Not to mention, a woman didn't get taut abs and a stellar behind from sitting around.

The knock propelled Cassidy to her feet. As she covered the last few feet to the door, she realized she was already smiling. She brought the smile under control and opened the door.

"Welcome, Duggan family." She made a sweeping bow which sent the girls into giggles.

"You look lovely." Tim stepped forward. For a second she thought he was going to kiss her. Then, as if he felt two pairs of curious eyes on him, he settled for squeezing her shoulder.

"Let me grab my keys and—"

A buzzer sounded from his pocket and the girls groaned.

Cassidy cocked her head and stared at them. "It's just a phone call."

"It's the hospital," Esther informed her.

Ellyn expelled a heavy sigh. "Someone is having a baby."

Tim slipped the phone from his pocket and answered. "Dr. Duggan."

Cassidy and the girls waited during the question-and-answer session. Something was obviously wrong. She could see it in the sudden tense set of Tim's shoulders and the lines of worry edging his brow.

"I'll be there right away. Get her prepped." After answering several more questions, Tim ended the call and slipped the phone back into his pocket.

"I'm afraid I have to head to the hospital." His apologetic gaze met Cassidy's. "I have a patient who needs immediate surgery."

"Don't go, Daddy." Esther grabbed his arm. "Not today. We're going to ride our bikes."

Tim's expression softened when he saw the distress on his daughter's face.

He squatted down in front of the two girls, taking their hands. "I'm as disappointed as both of you. But I have no choice. This woman needs me."

"Okay, Daddy," Ellyn said.

Esther grudgingly nodded.

Rising to his feet, he turned to Cassidy. "I'm sorry about this."

She gave an exaggerated sigh. "Some guys will do anything to avoid a bike ride."

That brought a smile to his gorgeous mouth.

"What about us?" Esther inched closer to Cassidy.

Tim pulled out the phone he'd just pocketed. "I'll see if Aunt Lindsey can watch you."

Cassidy put a hand on his arm. "They can stay here with me, if that's okay with you."

She wasn't sure what made her offer. After all, if they left she'd have the whole afternoon to herself. She could run errands, take a nap or do half a dozen other things she hadn't had time to do this week. Instead she'd willingly offered to watch two seven-year-olds? Had she lost her mind?

Tim appeared oddly touched by the offer. "Are you sure you don't mind?"

"Not at all," Cassidy said and was rewarded by squeals of delight. "We'll have fun."

## Chapter Thirteen

It was nearly seven by the time Tim returned to Cassidy's apartment. He was bone weary but satisfied with his patient's postsurgical condition.

As he climbed the stairs to her door, he realized that he hadn't given a single thought to the girls' welfare. Despite the sudden look of panic in Cassidy's eyes when she'd said goodbye, he knew she was up to the challenge.

He paused outside the door, listening to the giggles and laughter coming from inside the small apartment. He'd called when he was leaving the hospital to let Cassidy know he was on his way.

To his surprise, she'd sounded cheery and told him there was no need to rush. She and the girls were busy preparing dinner.

He hadn't quite known what to make of her buoyant mood. Caro had been into routines and schedules. Unexpected events had always thrown her into a bad mood. Because the life of an OB was filled with unexpected events, those bad moods had been frequent occurrences. Especially once he joined a practice where the doctors delivered their own babies.

Though Tim fully agreed with the philosophy of the practice, Caro had been pushing him to find a group where he would only be called to deliver when he was the doctor on call.

Though the disruption to their family life had caused problems in his marriage, Tim had been unwilling to even consider making a change. Looking back, he couldn't believe he'd been so hardheaded.

He'd known Caro's personality when he married her. She craved routine. Her suggestion was a compromise. Yet, he'd been unwilling to budge, to meet her halfway.

Shame flooded him.

Pushing the guilt and memories aside, he knocked.

"Come in," he heard Cassidy call. "It's unlocked."

*Only in Jackson Hole*, Tim thought, twisting the knob and pushing the door open. The second he stepped inside, the delicious scent of spiced meat assailed his nostrils. It appeared Cassidy was no longer bothered by certain smells.

"Daddy, Daddy." Esther came running and flung her arms around him. "We made taco pizza for dinner."

"And donut kebabs." Ellyn was, as usual, one step behind her sister.

"Taco pizza and donut kebabs," Tim repeated, but his mind wasn't on the food. It was on the streaks of bright color running through his daughters' light brown hair. "Your hair looks…colorful."

Hardly a precise word, but he was having difficulty coming up with better as he stared at the strands of purple and pink in Esther's hair and red and bright blue in Ellyn's.

"It's temporary," Cassidy said as she walked into the room. "Washes out."

Esther puffed with pride and tossed her head, sending the colorful strands back and forth.

"We had a color party." Ellyn stuck out her hand and her nails shimmered in the light all gold and silver. "Cassidy painted our nails and toes with glitter polish."

"I can see that. Very pretty." It was, Tim realized. Different, but pretty. What he really liked seeing were their wide smiles and bubbling enthusiasm.

Sometimes it seemed as if they were too serious for seven-year-olds. Then again, what did he know about such things?

All he knew was they'd obviously had a good day.

"Did I hear something about food?" He glanced at Cassidy and noticed her hair, which had been loosely flowing to her shoulder and was now in a rather odd-looking braid. "Your hair looks different, too."

Even as she smiled, her eyes flashed a warning. "After our color party I taught the girls how to braid and they practiced on my hair. I think they did an excellent job."

"Very nice." He gave the tail a tug and she yelped.

Tim smiled and glanced at the twins. "Your Aunt Lindsey used to make that sound whenever I pulled on her tail."

The girls giggled.

"Esi." Cassidy focused her attention on Esther. "How about you put place mats on the table? They're in the cupboard over there."

She pointed to a lower cupboard before turning her attention to Ellyn. "Elle, you know where the silverware is. What do you think we'll need for our food? A fork, for sure."

Ellyn thought for a second. "Maybe a knife?"

Cassidy appeared to consider. "Good call."

The girls hurried off to do their assigned tasks as Tim stared in amazement. He raised a brow. "Esi? Elle?"

Her lips quirked. "Every kid should have a nickname. Don't you agree, Doogie?"

He winced. *Doogie Howser, M.D.* had been a television series in syndication when he'd been younger. The main character was a young, geeky genius doctor. With the last name of Duggan, was it any wonder he'd been dubbed Doogie in middle school?

Tim tried to think back, to recall if Cassidy had ever had a nickname. "What was yours?"

A shadow passed over her pretty features and the light in her eyes dimmed. He wished he'd never asked.

"None I care to remember."

"I appreciate you watching the girls," he said.

"We had fun."

He inclined his head. "You sound surprised."

"I'm not good with kids."

"Who says?"

She lifted a shoulder then let it drop. "I never know what to say or the right thing to do."

More giggles came from the kitchen. "Sounds to me as if you did just fine. I'm sorry I had to leave and spoil our plans."

She looked at him, clearly puzzled. "It wasn't your fault. That woman needed you."

"Still—"

Her touch on his arm stopped the protest.

"Seriously," she said. "It's okay."

He raked a hand through his hair, gave a casual shrug. "Caro used to hate it when I was called away."

"She had two toddlers. She was probably just super stressed. I'm going to be stressed with just one. I'll be like, hey, what do I do now?" She gave a self-conscious little laugh, wishing she'd kept her mouth shut. "Keenan says I'll do just fine."

"Keenan McGregor?" Tim stilled. "You told him about the baby?"

Cassidy had made such a big deal of swearing him to silence and, as far as he knew, the only other one who knew she was pregnant was Lindsey, who'd been sworn to secrecy.

"Keenan and I, we go way back."

Tim remembered Keenan from high school. Like Cassidy, he and his sister, Betsy, had grown up in what Tim's mother referred to as the "bad" area of Jackson. He recalled seeing Cassidy at Keenan's wedding last year. "When did you run into him?"

"At a party at the Spring Gulch Country Club Friday night," she said. "I was feeling stressed and when he asked what was wrong, I unloaded. Just like old times."

While he was glad she had a friend to talk with, Tim felt an irrational surge of jealousy that she'd shared her thoughts and fears with another man.

*If I'd been there…*

But he hadn't been there. He'd been struggling with his own worries. He'd hoped clarity would come more easily if he wasn't around Cassidy. When she was near, he wanted only one thing…her.

Though Tim had been firmly committed to remaining single until the girls were raised, there was now another child to consider…and a woman.

He wanted his child raised under the same roof with both a mother and a father. He wanted his daughters to grow up with their little brother or sister. He cared for Cassidy. He believed they could build a good life together.

Did he love her? It was much, much too soon to even think about love. But he cared about her and wanted her to be happy. If she married him, he would do his best to be a good husband.

"Keenan says I have the ability to do anything I set my mind to," he heard Cassidy say.

Tim realized that while his mind had been traveling down unfamiliar roads, she'd continued to talk…about Keenan.

"And what did Mitzi think about you monopolizing her husband for the evening?"

He knew the words were a mistake the second they left his mouth. By then it was too late to pull them back.

Her eyes flashed blue fire. "Well, for starters I didn't monopolize him. And Mitzi understands we're old friends. He's like my big brother."

"Forget I said anything." Tim waved a dismissive hand. "What did you say we're having for dinner again?"

"Taco pizza," she said.

"Sounds nutritious."

Her blue eyes could have frozen boiling water. "Actually, I got the recipe from a children's website."

"Would this be the same place you got the recipe for donut kebabs?" he said in a flippant tone.

Tim wasn't sure what was wrong with him. Why did he feel the urge to needle her? But when he thought of her and Keenan…

She laughed suddenly, a loud booming laugh. "You're jealous."

"I am not," he said indignantly.

"Are, too." She smirked. "You're jealous of Keenan. A married man."

Tim scowled. He almost retorted "am not" but thankfully pulled the words just in time, the retort too similar to what he heard when the girls bickered.

Cassidy's expression turned serious and she took a step forward, resting her hand on his arm, her blue eyes warm. "Keenan is one of the few people on this planet who truly understands what it was like for me growing up. He knows the fears that come from such an upbringing. I trust him."

The knife that had lodged in his heart twisted at her words.

"You can trust me, too, Cassidy." He took a step closer. "Just like Keenan is there for you, I want to be someone you can come to with your fears and concerns."

"I believe you mean that."

"I do."

When she smiled, an emotion Tim couldn't quite identify shimmered in the air between them, warming his heart and dislodging the knife's hold.

She patted his cheek. "Thanks."

He pulled her to him, brushing his lips across hers, experiencing a surge of relief when she wound her arms around his neck.

"Forgive me for acting like a jerk?"

"I might need a little more convincing." She lifted her face upward and her lips parted in invitation.

Tim lowered his head.

"The oven dinged," Esther announced. "Can I get the pizza?"

He and Cassidy sprang apart.

"Thanks for offering, sweetie," Cassidy said, sounding remarkably composed. "But that pan is monster heavy. I'd love some help, though."

Tim watched his little girl's face light up. He recalled the last time she'd offered to help at his mother's house. Suzanne liked everything just so and had sent Esther and her sister out to play.

"Wash your hands." Cassidy gave Tim a playful shove. "Then hurry back because dinner will be on the table pronto."

"Yes, ma'am," he said, then surprised them all by giving Cassidy a quick kiss before hurrying down the hall with a lift in his step.

Esi giggled. "Daddy kissed you."

Puzzled, Cassidy brought her hand to her lips. "Yes, he did."

"Silly Daddy."

Cassidy smiled and took the child's hand, swinging it between them. "Let's get the pizza."

"And the donuts," Ellyn called out. "Those are my favorite."

The next day Tim was able to leave the clinic right at five. The day was bright and sunny. He'd promised to take his daughters to the park for a picnic to make up for the missed bike ride yesterday.

When he'd had a break in patient appointments earlier, he'd tried to reach Cassidy. He hoped to convince her to change her mind about joining them for the picnic. But his call went straight to voice mail.

Yesterday, she'd mentioned her Monday was "crazy" busy but he recalled her last appointment was at five, so there was still hope. Once he picked up the girls, he'd try to reach her again. The possibility of seeing her tonight had him whistling as he strode up the sidewalk to the front porch of his parents' home.

"Someone is in a good mood." His dad straightened from where he'd been pruning a bush that needed no trimming. Ever since his father had retired last year, he'd been trying to find some rhythm to his life.

Steve Duggan golfed and played tennis with friends at the club but that only filled so many hours in a day. Though Tim sometimes felt guilty over his parents watching the girls, he knew they enjoyed it.

Tim paused at the bottom of the steps next to where his father stood. "It was a good day. How's it been for you?"

An emotion Tim couldn't immediately decipher darkened his dad's eyes. "Difficult."

Tim cocked his head.

His father ran a hand across the face that was an older version of his own. "Sarah."

It was all he needed to say. Tim wondered how he could have forgotten the anniversary of his sister's death from leukemia. She'd been stricken her freshman year and the doctors had never been able to get her into remission.

Though it had been over a decade since his beautiful, vibrant sister had passed, he still missed her sunny smile. She'd had the same love of life he so admired in Cassidy.

"I wish I'd remembered." Guilt sluiced through Tim. "I'd have made other arrangements for the girls today."

"Then I'm glad you didn't," Steve said. "I enjoy having them here. They're like two rays of sunshine."

"What about mother? How's she doing?"

His dad hesitated.

Though their mother had borne three children, Sarah had always been their mother's favorite. The favoritism hadn't bothered Tim, but living in Sarah's shadow had been hard on Lindsey. Only in recent years had his younger sister found happiness and contentment in her life.

Tim focused on his father. "What kind of mood is she in?"

His dad's lips tipped in a slight smile. "Loaded for bear."

Tim grimaced. "That bad?"

His dad nodded. "My advice. Grab the girls and get the hell out of Dodge."

"Appreciate the warning."

Still, making a quick getaway proved impossible. The twins were in the middle of an art project on the dining room table, which his mother said would only take fifteen more minutes to complete. In the meantime, she requested he speak with her on the back patio.

Tim followed her outside, refusing her offer of a glass of iced tea. Just gazing at her set jaw and tight lips, he knew *loaded for* bear had been too mild. His mother was spoiling for a fight.

She crossed her arms across her chest and turned to face him, lifting her chin. "You might be angry with me when I tell you, but I don't care. I did what I thought was best."

"Well, that certainly gets my attention." Tim kept his tone easy even as a feeling of dread rose inside him.

"I went to see that woman today."

His blood turned to ice. "What woman would that be?"

She waved her hand in an agitated motion. "That Cassidy creature."

Tim glanced at her hair. Though he was no expert, it looked pretty much the same as it had that morning. "You needed a haircut?"

"I went to voice my displeasure over how she took care of my granddaughters yesterday." Suzanne shot Tim an accusing glance. "I would have changed my plans if I'd known you needed someone to watch them. But you didn't call."

Ignoring the last part of her diatribe, Tim focused on the first section. "What did you say to Cassidy?"

If Suzanne noticed the sudden chill in his tone it didn't show.

"I told her that taco pizza and donut kebabs were totally inappropriate for a growing child's nutrition. Then—" his mother exhaled a frustrated breath "—I moved on to the hair and nails. My granddaughters are not strumpets. They are growing up in a decent, God-fearing home. I made it clear I won't have them looking like white trash."

Tim's gut constricted. "Tell me you're joking."

Suzanne looked affronted. "I most certainly am not. If you don't care how your daughters eat and—"

"Taco pizza," Tim interrupted, "that the girls made themselves. You used to make pizza, though God knows we were never allowed to help."

His mother flinched as if he'd slapped her.

"The pizza I could have overlooked." She lifted her chin even higher. "But *donut* kebabs? The girls rattled on and on about how good they were. They didn't even care about the blueberry muffins I'd made them this morning."

And that, no doubt, was part of this. "Did you ask the girls what was in the donut kebabs?"

She sniffed. "I believe the name is self-explanatory."

"Actually, they contain only very small bites of donut." Tim fought to hold on to his temper. "Most of the kebab is fruit on a skewer. Blackberries and strawberries primarily. And did the twins tell you about the salad in a mason jar they made? Ellyn, who doesn't even like lettuce, ate all of hers last night."

"She should have told me."

"I'm sure either of the twins would have told you if you'd asked. They—"

"I'm not talking about them," his mother said dismissively. "I'm referring to the woman you kissed in front of your daughters."

*Ah, now we're getting down to it*, Tim thought with a resigned sigh. "I'm an adult, Mother. I don't have to have your approval to kiss a woman."

"Oh, Tim, what were you—"

"My actions aren't on trial here, Mother. Tell me what you said to Cassidy." His tone brooked no argument.

"I hardly think—"

"Tell me what you said."

"That I was shocked you would let someone like her, so obviously incapable of taking care of children, be in charge." Suzanne hesitated, her eyes searching Tim's. "She dyed their hair."

"It washes out," he said flatly.

"I believe it's entirely inappropriate for girls that age

to wear nail polish." Suzanne lifted her chin. "I didn't let Sarah wear nail polish until…"

Tears filled his mother's eyes, but Tim was too angry to care. "What did Cassidy say to you?"

"She told me to leave." His mother gave a disbelieving laugh. "Looked me right in the eye and told me she was glad she wasn't part of my family. Can you believe the nerve?"

Tim's heart sank. If Cassidy was glad she wasn't part of his mother's family, that could mean only one thing.

She wouldn't want to ever be part of *his* family, either. At this moment, he didn't blame her.

## Chapter Fourteen

The bike ride with Tim and the twins to Snow King Mountain and back to Jackson gave Cassidy plenty of time to reflect on the past weeks.

Last Sunday had been a good day. She'd enjoyed having the twins over. After the "color" party, she'd looked up some kid-friendly recipes on the internet.

The twins had been hesitant when she'd first invited them to help her. It was almost as if they feared doing something wrong. But they quickly realized in *her* kitchen there was no wrong, only interesting twists and turns.

Dinner had been fun and Tim had seemed pleased by the girls' happiness. Cassidy had begun to feel that maybe she didn't suck at this mother thing after all. Then, on Monday, when she was still riding a high, Suzanne had stopped by the shop.

*White trash.* The woman didn't want her granddaughters to be white trash.

Cassidy hadn't let her see she'd drawn blood. In fact,

when she'd ordered Tim's mother from her shop in a low, pleasant voice, she'd felt immensely proud of herself for keeping her cool.

But she'd be lying if she didn't admit to herself that the words had cut to the heart of her fears. At the time, contacting Tim didn't even occur to her. What would be the point? Suzanne was his mother and, worst of all, she was right.

Country club and white trash didn't mix.

She could only imagine what Suzanne would think when she found out that this piece of white trash was carrying her grandchild.

Tim had apologized profusely for his mother's behavior. Cassidy had told him it was no big deal and brushed aside his concern. After all, she'd been dealing with this kind of thing all her life.

There had been a time, a very short time, when she'd first opened her salon that she'd considered trying to be country club. But she knew it would be futile. She liked wild hair and flashy clothes. What was that saying? *You could take the girl out of the trailer park but you couldn't take the trailer park out of the girl.*

Besides, she refused to live her life simply to please someone else. After she'd graduated from high school and had been free of her mother once and for all, she'd been determined to live life on her own terms. That was what she'd done, and quite successfully, for over a decade.

She'd gotten her degree in business through online courses and become a success. She hadn't stumbled. Not once.

Until Tim Duggan.

Getting pregnant had been a serious detour in the wrong direction. Though she'd never been tempted to do anything but continue the pregnancy, she had to admit she'd railed against God for letting something like this happen to her.

They'd used protection. Why did it have to be her that got caught?

Still, she'd learned long ago she'd never get ahead by wishing things were different. It was what it was.

Suzanne had made Cassidy realize that she'd been foolishly hoping for more in terms of Tim and the girls. There had been a moment on Sunday when she'd actually found herself wondering what it would be like if they were a family. What it would be like to have Tim come home every night...

Because she'd been angry—and hurt—by his mother's behavior, Cassidy had been tempted to break off all contact with Tim. But that would have been an emotion-driven decision. He was not his mother's keeper, and more important, Tim was her baby's father. As he'd said on more than one occasion, it would be easier for everyone if they got to know each other better before the baby was born.

So, they'd agreed that she'd have dinner with Tim and the twins a couple of times during the week. The Saturdays that she didn't have a wedding, they'd spend time with the girls during the day, then she and Tim would go out at night.

The twelve-week mark loomed before her. A date Cassidy approached with both relief and dread.

Relief because it meant the chance of a miscarriage dropped to less than 5 percent. Dread because it meant choosing a doctor and telling the world she'd gotten herself knocked up.

Though the twins continued to beg, Cassidy didn't put color in their hair or paint their nails. Still, she enjoyed the girls and felt a bond with them that surprised her.

Today they'd decided on a bike ride. Tim hadn't thought the girls could keep up, but Cassidy had assured him the girls were stronger than he thought.

Now, after parking their bikes, they strolled the downtown sidewalks looking for a place to eat. The fact that they were dressed for biking limited their options but there were still plenty of choices.

"Can we eat at Hill of Beans, please?" Esther begged when the popular eatery came into view.

"Sounds good to me." Cassidy slanted a glance at Tim. *His girls. His choice.*

"Works for me." Tim opened the door.

They ordered at the counter and were looking for a place to sit when Jayne and her mother walked in. From the bags in their hands, it appeared the two women had spent their morning shopping.

"Paula. Jayne." Tim's smile was warm and friendly. "Nice to see you both."

"Why don't we all sit together?" Paula paused as if noticing Cassidy for the first time.

Before responding, Tim caught Cassidy's eye.

She gave a noncommittal shrug.

"Sounds good." Tim glanced around the dining room. "The large table in the corner should work."

Cassidy sat between the girls and watched Jayne hesitantly take a seat next to Tim.

"I was telling my mother that the task force is making real progress." Jayne took a dainty sip of her Italian soda. "Cassidy is a terrific leader. She keeps us focused. Though I'm sure it sometimes feels like herding cats."

Before Tim could say a word, Paula jumped into the conversation. "Did you know Jayne is in the running for an award given to top media specialists?"

Tim glanced at Jayne. "I didn't. Congratulations."

"The black-and-white ball is coming up." Paula took a sip of her cappuccino and slanted a glance at Cassidy before shifting her attention to Tim. "I hope you're planning to attend. Jayne tells me you're an excellent dancer."

Cassidy remembered seeing Tim and Jayne dance together. They'd looked as if they belonged together.

"What do you say, Cass?" Tim fixed warm hazel eyes on her. "Got a black or white dress in that colorful closet of yours?"

"Fancy country-club stuff isn't for me. I'm more of a beer and two-step kind of gal." Cassidy could have cheered that her voice came out casual and offhand, just as she'd intended.

Tim surprised her by reaching over and taking her hand, bringing it to his lips for a kiss that made the girls giggle. "Well, we'll just have to ask the orchestra if they'll play a two-step."

Her heart, she was ashamed to admit, simply melted.

A momentary stillness settled over the table, finally broken by one of the twins telling Paula about the time Cassidy had put colored streaks in their hair.

"We looked real pretty," Esther said with a decisive nod.

"We had glitter polish, too," Ellyn added.

Cassidy guessed she shouldn't have been surprised that the twins had brought up the subject. Every time she saw them they asked when they could have another color party. She put them off, the words *white trash* ringing in her ears.

"I wish I could have seen you with the color in your hair," Jayne told the girls, then shifted her attention to Cassidy. "I've always thought it'd be fun to put a streak of color in my hair."

"Just name the time and date." Cassidy almost laughed at the look of shock on Paula's face. "I can do any color you like."

Jayne tapped a finger against her lips. "I'd like to do it before school is back in session. Perhaps—"

"You can't be serious," Paula interrupted.

"Why not?" Jayne asked.

"You know the kind of people who do those kinds of things—" Paula appeared to notice the bright blue streak in Cassidy's hair and paused. "I'm sorry. I just meant that while it may be pretty, it's sort of—"

"White trashy?" Cassidy filled in the blank.

"Exactly," Paula said quickly, then stopped, chagrined.

Esther cocked her head. "What does *white trashy* mean?"

"That isn't a nice word," Tim told his daughter, his eyes hard. "Isn't that right, Paula?"

"Absolutely right," the older woman said immediately, looking abashed.

"If you can fit me in on Monday at four," Jayne continued, as if the interruption hadn't occurred, "I'd love to get a cut also."

After checking the calendar on her phone, Cassidy nodded. "That'll work."

The conversation continued without incident and when they rose to leave, Paula's hand curved around Cassidy's arm. "May I speak with you a moment?"

Cassidy hesitated. She wasn't a coward but neither was she a masochist. Out of the corner of her eye, she saw Tim's concerned gaze.

*Suck it up*, Cassidy told herself and straightened her shoulders. "Certainly."

The two women stepped away from the others.

"I'm sorry if I said anything to offend you," Paula began.

Well, this was a pleasant surprise.

"No offense taken."

"It's just that I'm conservative." Two bright swaths of pink colored Paula's cheeks. "You understand."

"Of course."

Cassidy understood all right. She just wondered how often she had to be beaten over the head with the truth for it to finally sink in that she and Tim came from different worlds.

Cassidy could tell Tim wanted to discuss the incident with Paula and Jayne but the girls were in the backseat, listening to their every word. Then, when they pulled up to Tim's home, Suzanne and Steve were waiting on the porch.

"I'm sorry about stopping by unexpectedly." Tim's father shot a look that managed to be both apologetic and sympathetic in Cassidy's direction.

A chill traveled up her spine.

"I need to speak with you." Suzanne spoke stiffly, her gaze only on her son.

"What's this about, Mother?"

"It's something best discussed in private."

Though Cassidy wasn't a big fan of Suzanne Duggan, the woman looked as if she was about to cry. Cassidy hoped for Tim's sake that Suzanne didn't have any health issues. She knew how much Tim and the girls loved the woman.

"If you need to speak with your parents," Cassidy said, assuming Suzanne would want her husband with her when she told her son her news, "I can take the girls into the backyard. It's been a while since I've played on swings."

"Yippee!" Esther jumped in the air.

"Thanks." Tim squeezed her shoulder.

He watched Cassidy and his daughters disappear around the corner of the house. Then, to his surprise, his father followed them.

Tim cocked his head. "What's up? Is something wrong?"

"Yes." Suzanne's voice shook and tears welled in her eyes. "Something is very, very wrong."

Quickly moving to his mother's side, Tim put an arm around her and sat beside her on the top step. "Tell me."

"Oh, Tim, what were you thinking?"

What was he thinking? Tim pulled his brows together. "I'm thinking I'm worried about you."

"You should be worried about yourself."

Still confused, Tim forced a little laugh. "I'm doing just fine. In fact, I couldn't be better."

Her gaze searched his face. "You don't have to pretend with me. I know you must be devastated."

Tim felt a prickle of unease travel up his spine. "About what?"

"I know Cassidy is pregnant. Your sister let it slip." Suzanne pressed her lips together. "Can you believe Lindsey is actually excited about this travesty? She told me she can't wait for the two cousins to be old enough to play together."

"Lindsey always was a planner." It was an inane thing to say, but this conversation had caught him off guard.

"Don't you try to distract me." Suzanne shifted on the front step to more fully face him. "I realize I told you to have your fun with her, if that's what you needed, but I warned you to take precautions to avoid unintended consequences."

"I wouldn't describe a baby as an unintended consequence." His words held a biting edge.

His mother gave a humorless laugh that somehow managed to sound a little sad. "I didn't want this for you. And, if you're being honest with me and yourself, you can't say that you wanted it, either."

Tim paused. No, he couldn't say that he'd been ready for another child, or for a relationship. But Cassidy had exploded into his life and blown his plans sky-high. Lately, he'd realized it had all been for the better.

Before her, he'd lived his life in shades of gray and brown. Not that there was anything wrong with a life lived on an even keel, any more than there was with sailing on a day with a gentle breeze. It was pleasant.

But there was something about bright colors and loud laughter that made the boat ride exhilarating. No, though what had happened definitely hadn't been in his plans, he didn't have regrets.

Apparently taking his silence for assent, Suzanne plowed ahead.

She reached out and laid her hand on his arm, her voice soft and low, her eyes filled with compassion. "Although your father and I taught you to take responsibility for your mistakes, I don't want you to martyr yourself because you let this woman seduce you."

Cassidy seduce him? He laughed. "She didn't seduce me. If anything, it was the other way around."

"Do your best by the child," Suzanne said, dismissing his comments. "But don't marry her. There are some women you sleep with, some you marry. Jayne is the kind of woman you should marry. Don't just think about you, Tim. Think about the twins. Jayne would make the perfect mother for your children. Can you say the same thing about Cassidy?"

"Yes." Tim met his mother's searching gaze with a steady one of his own. "Cassidy is great with the girls. I have no doubts she'll be a fabulous mother to our baby. I'm beginning to realize she's the best thing that ever happened to me."

As Tim uttered the words, he realized they were true.

*I didn't want this for you. And, if you're being honest with me and yourself, you can't say that you wanted it ,either.*

Cassidy paused at the corner of the house. She hadn't meant to eavesdrop… Okay, so maybe she had. But she'd had a reason for coming around the corner. She'd left her phone in the car. Cassidy had paused and stayed out of sight when she'd heard Suzanne speaking and realized she was the topic du jour.

She wasn't sure what she expected to hear, but it wasn't the pounding silence to his mother's question. Then again, she had wanted to know where Tim stood.

Now she had her answer. She whirled and ran straight into Steve.

"Whoa." He grabbed her arms, steadying her when she might have fallen. "You move as fast as Esther and Ellyn."

His eyes were warm and kind and filled with concern. He looked so much like his son that her heart twisted in her chest and tears filled her eyes. But she hurriedly blinked them back before Steve could see.

"I just remembered there's someplace I need to be."

"Well, then, let me get Tim——"

"No." She nearly shouted the word, then lowered her voice and took a deep breath. "He and your wife seem to be having a heavy-duty discussion."

"I know Suz hasn't been herself since Lindsey stopped over earlier." Lines of worry furrowed his brow. "She wouldn't tell me what she needed to speak with Tim about, only that it was urgent."

He raised a questioning brow as if hoping she'd supply the answer.

"I have no idea," she lied. "They simply seem really focused."

Steve looked as if he didn't quite believe her, but let it drop.

"My wife is a good woman," he told her. "She gets a little intense at times. Goes off in left field. But she always comes around."

Though she appreciated Steve's kindness, Cassidy gave a casual shrug. "I really need to take off. I assume you'll keep an eye on the girls?"

"Sure." He shoved his hands into his pockets. "I'll happily take you wherever you need to go. The girls can come with us. They love car rides."

"Not necessary." Cassidy flashed him a bright smile. "My friends live just down the street. I, ah, told them I planned to stop by. They'll take me home."

"What friends are those?" Steve asked conversationally, though his eyes remained intense.

Crap. A direct question.

"Mitzi and Keenan McGregor." Then, because she feared Tim and his mother might conclude their conversation any moment, Cassidy impulsively rose on her tiptoes and gave Steve a kiss on the cheek. "You've been very kind to me. I appreciate it."

Those eyes, so much like Tim's, bored into hers. "You're good for my son. I don't recall ever seeing him this happy."

Cassidy gave a short wave then turned in the direction of the walkway that ran behind the properties on this block.

As she quickened her steps, Cassidy told herself she wasn't running away. She was making a conscious decision, a rational choice, one in her best interests.

But as she broke into a light jog, even she wasn't convinced.

## Chapter Fifteen

Mitzi McGregor opened the front door to her home and smiled in welcome. "Cassidy. What a pleasant surprise. Come in."

Somehow managing to look stylish in cargo shorts and a sage-colored tee, Mitzi motioned her inside. The daughter of a Mexican mother and Argentinian father, Mitzi had skin the color of café au lait, light brown hair streaked with blond and bright blue eyes, a very pleasing combination.

She was smart and spunky and could hold her own against Keenan, whom Cassidy knew could be a bit headstrong and bossy at times. While on paper a talented orthopedic surgeon and ex-con pilot might seem an odd match, Mitzi and Keenan were perfect for each other.

"I, ah." Cassidy hesitated and found her thoughts returning to Suzanne's words, to Tim's silence, and emotion made her heart swell to bursting. She swiped away a few tears that dared to fall. "I was in the neighborhood and thought I'd—"

"Oh, honey." Concern filled Mitzi's cobalt-blue eyes and she put an arm around her waist as she ushered her inside. "Can I get you something? A glass of water or—"

"Who was at the door?" Keenan came into the room and quickly took note of his wife's furrowed brow and Cassidy wiping away tears. He glanced around as if searching for the cause of her distress. "What's wrong?"

"I was wondering if one of you could give me a ride home."

"I'll give you a ride home," a deep masculine voice behind her said. "If that's what you want."

*Tim.*

Cassidy closed her eyes and prayed for strength. When she opened them, the tears were gone. She turned. "Thanks. I've got it covered."

His gaze searched hers. "We need to talk."

Keenan stepped forward, putting himself between her and Tim. "Not until I'm certain she wants to speak with you."

Tim felt his temper rise. Not only had he been forced to deal with his mother, he'd gone to the back to find Cassidy gone. Thankfully, his father had a clue where she might be.

Now it looked as if he'd have to go through Keenan to get to Cassidy. Tim tightened his jaw. Though he'd never been a brawler, far from it in fact, no one was standing between him and Cassidy. Not even her old *friend*.

"Stay out of this, McGregor," Tim growled. "This is between Cassidy and me."

"You seem to forget this is my house, Doogie." Keenan's eyes were hard as steel. "And I don't recall inviting you here."

"Oh, for goodness' sake." Mitzi pushed in between the two men. "As much as I love a little excitement, this is ridiculous."

She slipped a hand around her husband's muscular biceps. "It's obvious Cassidy and Tim need to talk."

When Keenan opened his mouth to protest, Mitzi hurriedly spoke. "You know as well as I do that Cassidy can handle herself. She's tough. And—"

Mitzi met Cassidy's gaze. "We'll be right in the kitchen if you need us."

Cassidy gave a slight nod.

Though still grumbling, Keenan let his pretty wife tug him out of the room.

"If I didn't know better, I'd think there was something between the two of you."

Cassidy shot him a sharp gaze.

"Just trying to lighten the mood." Tim lifted his hands palm sides out but then the joking expression fled his face and his expression turned serious. "I guess I hoped if you needed something, someone, I'd be the guy you ran to, not Keenan."

Though he did a good job of hiding it, Cassidy heard the undercurrent of hurt in the words. Despite their best efforts, they kept hurting each other. And that she couldn't abide.

The phone in his pocket rang. He ignored it.

She gestured to the sofa. "You want to talk. Let's talk."

He expelled an audible breath. "I was hoping you'd say that."

When she sat on the burgundy leather couch facing the fireplace, Tim took a seat beside her.

"Why did you leave?" he asked.

"I heard what your mother said." Honesty, she told herself, was the best policy. "And frankly I agree with her. I'm not the kind of woman you should marry. I wouldn't be a good mother to your daughters, Tim. Heck, I even worry about being a good mother to my own child."

He opened his mouth to say something then appeared to reconsider. After a moment, he spoke. "Tell me how you feel. About me. About the girls."

He was so analytical, so logical. Unlike her mother and her mother's various boyfriends, Tim didn't fly off the handle or shout or scream or get emotional.

She would show him the same consideration.

"I've told you a little of how I grew up. Crystal was the opposite of what a good mother should be. Despite my best efforts, I tend to be more impulsive, to be less controlled than I probably should be."

"I tend to be too controlled," Tim admitted. "I believe that's why we're so good together. You bring out a side in me I didn't even know I had, and it's a good thing."

"You'll get tired of me."

"Who says?"

"I'm not the kind of woman you should marry."

"You're exactly the kind of woman I should marry."

His phone rang again, the sound shrill in the silence.

"Don't you need to get that?" she asked. "It could be the hospital."

He shook his head. A muscle in his jaw jumped. "It's my mother's ringtone."

Regardless of what her husband thought, Suzanne wouldn't come around. She'd never accept a relationship with Cassidy and her son. Tim was close to his family. His daughters loved their grandparents. She wouldn't be responsible for breaking that family apart.

Cassidy met his gaze. "I don't know if you're familiar with the words of a Kenny Rogers song that says 'You have to know when to hold 'em, know when to fold 'em.' Well, we've given it a good try, Tim."

"We haven't given it a good try." Tim's tone took on urgency as he leaned forward. "We've played at building a relationship. You're scared to commit, Cassidy, I get that. You don't want to be hurt. You don't want to hurt me. And you don't want the girls hurt."

"Exactly," she said, relieved he finally seemed to get it.

"But we have a baby to consider." He paused as if wanting the words to sink in. "I believe it's time to get serious, to fully commit to making a relationship between us work."

"What are you saying?"

"I want you to marry me."

"Marry you?" Cassidy choked out the words. "That seems a bit drastic."

"I want our child to have my name. I'm traditional enough that I want us to be married when he or she is born."

"But marriage is a huge step." Though Cassidy hardly considered herself a romantic, she wanted more than he was offering.

"We have a baby coming," he reminded her. "Marriage is the responsible choice."

*Responsible.* After the chaos of what she'd grown up in, she'd sworn she would do her best to live a responsible lifestyle. But she'd also been determined to only marry for love.

Where did that leave her now?

*Right behind the eight ball.*

Keenan appeared in the doorway. Apparently Mitzi had only been successful in keeping him at bay for so long. But the sight of the weeping woman behind him had them both jumping to their feet.

"Mom, what's wrong?" Tim crossed the living room in several long strides, caught her arms and supported her as she swayed.

"It's Esther," she managed to choke out. "It was an accident. She fell from the tree—"

The woman broke into weeping sobs.

Cassidy froze at the despair in Suzanne's eyes.

Tim shook her. "Tell me what happened. Where's Esther now?"

"The ambulance came. She's on her way to the hospital." Suzanne lifted her tear-drenched eyes to meet his. "I'm so sorry. I tried to call you but—"

His mother never had a chance to finish what she was about to say. Tim shoved her into Keenan's startled arms then raced out the door and sprinted toward the car with Cassidy on his heels.

Not until the hospital was in sight did it occur to Cassidy that they'd driven off without Suzanne. She kept the pleasant thought to herself. Right now Tim didn't need any distractions.

With his foot heavy on the gas pedal and his hands clenching the steering wheel in a death grip, he was totally focused on getting to the hospital in record time.

"She'll be fine." Cassidy spoke confidently, hoping to stanch her own fear. "She's a super-strong girl."

He didn't respond.

She wasn't sure he even heard her.

He wheeled the SUV into a parking space adjacent to the ER. The vehicle had barely come to a stop when Tim slammed it into Park and jerked the keys from the ignition. He flung open the door and covered the distance to the sliding glass doors in ground-eating strides.

Cassidy trotted to keep up.

The gray-haired woman at the reception desk looked up when the doors slid open and they burst into the waiting area.

"Esther Duggan." Tim snapped the name. "Where is she?"

"Tim."

He whirled at the sound of his father's voice. "How is she? Where is she?"

Steve rose from the seats where he and Ellyn had been sitting, her hand nestled in his. "She's in radiology. They told me as soon as they were finished I could go back and be with her."

"What's wrong with her?"

Steve blinked, clearly flummoxed by the question.

"All Suzanne told us was that Esther had fallen and was on her way to the hospital." Cassidy spoke quickly, knowing Tim was ready to tear the place apart to locate his daughter.

"She climbed the backyard tree and fell." Though his eyes were filled with worry, his father's tone gave no evidence of distress. "It appears her arm is broken. She was in a lot of pain. We're not sure how hard she hit her head. We thought it best to call an ambulance."

Cassidy could almost see Tim's mind working, processing the information. He briefly glanced at his daughter. When he spoke again to his father, his tone was calmer. "Did the bone come through the skin? Did she lose consciousness?"

"No, the bone didn't break the skin." Steve shook his head for extra emphasis. "In terms of the second, we don't think so. If she did, it was only for a short time. David said he'd check for signs of a concussion."

"David?"

"David Wahl." Steve's lips lifted slightly. "I was happy to see he was on duty."

Dr. David Wahl, head of the Emergency Medicine Department, had been a friend of Tim's since childhood.

As if saying his name had conjured him up, David strolled into the waiting area. His gaze fixed on Tim. "I thought I heard your voice out here."

Tim stepped forward. "How is she?"

"Mild concussion," the other doctor said, suddenly all business. "X-rays show a nondisplaced fractured humerus."

"The humerus is the bone that extends from the shoulder to the elbow," Tim informed his dad and Cassidy, his gaze never leaving David's face. "I'd like an ortho consult."

"Already anticipated that one. I have a call in to Bene-dict Campbell."

"No need. I'll take a look." Mitzi, also an orthopedic sur-geon and in the same practice as Ben Campbell, announced as she, her husband and Tim's mother came through the doors.

"That's my woman," Keenan said proudly. "One step inside a hospital and she takes over the place."

"I'd appreciate it, Mitzi." Tim slanted his gaze back to David. "Not to impugn your diagnostic—"

"No offense taken." David gestured to Tim. "I'll show you back to Esther now. Mitzi can examine her and re-view the X-rays. You can stay with her while she's casted, unless Mitzi feels for some reason surgery is indicated."

*Surgery.* A chill gripped Cassidy's heart and every inch of her body turned to ice.

"When I heard she was in an ambulance…" Tim took a deep breath and let it out slowly.

Cassidy closed her hand around his in a gesture of com-fort and found his fingers ice-cold, just like hers.

David glanced at the tablet in his hand. "Does Esther have any medication allergies?"

Tim shook his head. "None. She's a healthy girl."

"Is she on any medications?"

Tim shook his head.

David nodded. "That's what your father said, but I just wanted to be certain."

"I'll just wait—"

Cassidy started to step back but Tim's grasp tightened on her hand.

"She'll want to see you," he said.

Suzanne, who'd remained silent, started forward, but Steven took her arm.

"Stay here, Suz. Give Esther time with her father and Cassidy. Keep Ellyn and me company."

Cassidy saw Suzanne's mouth open, but she shut it without even a murmur of protest.

David led them down a long corridor. The walls were a pristine white. The floors had been buffed to a shiny gray so glossy, Cassidy swore she could see her reflection.

"The nurse will have some insurance and treatment forms for you to sign." David paused in front of room 112 and shifted his gaze from Tim to Mitzi. "Thanks for the assistance. I'll call Dr. Campbell and let him know you have things under control."

Mitzi winked. "Be sure and tell Ben he owes me."

David only laughed.

Though Cassidy expected Mitzi to immediately examine Esther, the doctor moved to where the X-rays were displayed. Cassidy wondered if she did it in order to give Tim some time with his daughter first.

The redheaded nurse in the room looked up from her charting. Cassidy bit back a groan. Leila Daltry, the woman who'd bid on Tim at the bachelor auction, stood to greet them.

"Dr. Duggan." Her smile dimmed when she saw Cassidy then her gaze snapped back to Tim. "Esther has been asking for you."

Tim gave her a cursory nod, his entire attention riveted to the bed where his daughter lay. The normally high-spirited girl looked pale and oh-so-small against the crisp white sheets. Her hair had come loose from the clip and formed a light brown halo on the pillow. She brightened immediately when she saw them.

"Hey, Es." Tim stepped close and caressed the side of her face with gentle fingers. "Cass and I came as soon as we heard. How are you feeling?"

Tears flooded her eyes. "Don't be mad, Daddy."

Confusion blanketed Tim's face. "I'm not mad. Why would I be mad?"

Esther dropped her gaze and her bottom lip trembled. "I climbed the tree."

"I'm not angry with you." Tim's voice grew thick with emotion. "I just want you better."

Cassidy moved closer. "That's what everyone wants."

"My arm hurts and my head, too." Tears slipped down Esther's cheeks. "I'm scared."

"Once you're home, I'll tell you all about the time I broke my arm." Cassidy forced an exaggerated sigh. "I wanted a pink cast in the worst way but back then the colored ones cost more so I got stuck with boring white."

"I want a pink cast." Esther's tears suddenly dried up and she cast a pleading glance at her father. "Can I have a pink cast?"

"I think that can be arranged." Tim looked as if he was fighting hard not to smile.

"Dr. Duggan, I have forms for you to sign." Leila smiled reassuringly at Esther. "Dr. McGregor has ordered some medicine to help with the pain in your arm."

Once Mitzi finished reviewing the X-rays and did her exam, it wasn't long before Esther sported a hot-pink cast on her left arm.

"I'm so jealous." Cassidy let her gaze linger on Esther's arm. "That is one cool color."

Tim shot her an appreciative smile and Cassidy was embarrassed to admit her heart melted.

Then, suddenly, the whole family was in the room, crowded around the little girl they all loved. When Ellyn asked if she could have one just like it, Tim only laughed.

## *Chapter Sixteen*

Normally Tuesdays rolled along at a comfortable pace. Though as a business owner Cassidy had a goal to fill all appointment slots all the time, she had to admit she was enjoying the breathing room today. It gave her the opportunity to order supplies and catch up on some bookkeeping.

Yet, despite the quiet of her "office" in the salon's back storage room, she hadn't been able to keep herself fully on task. Her mind kept circling back to Tim's marriage proposal on Saturday.

Marriage was the responsible choice, he'd asserted. He wanted the baby to have his name. Much of what he'd said made sense. But there hadn't been a single word about love anywhere in the mountain of words.

"Am I interrupting?"

Cassidy jerked her gaze to the doorway to discover Tim standing there. "How did you get back here?"

"Daffy pointed me in this direction." He lifted a hand. "Don't blame her. I told her you were expecting me."

Cassidy pulled her brows together, thought for a moment. "Did we have plans for this afternoon?"

"No." His smile flashed. "But I haven't seen you since Saturday and I desperately needed my Cassidy-fix."

That boyish smile combined with the knowledge that he'd missed her sent warmth rushing through her body. She rose to her feet and stretched. "I could use some exercise before my five o'clock arrives. Care to join me in a short walk?"

"Absolutely." His gaze lingered on the wavy strands of blond she'd streaked with copper yesterday. "I like the hair."

Though it pleased her that he'd noticed, she lifted a shoulder in a shrug. "It'll be different the next time you see me."

"Can't wait."

After speaking briefly with Daffodil, they left the shop and started down the sidewalk. Cassidy wasn't aware where she was headed until she reached the small park, encircled by a black wrought-iron gate, two blocks from her shop.

"Let's swing." She reached out and grabbed his hand, tugging him along.

"You weren't kidding when you told the twins you liked to swing."

"I never joke about important things." She glanced around the empty park. "It's such a beautiful day I thought this might be standing room only. Instead, we're the only ones here."

"Probably because it's a weekday and closing in on the supper hours."

"That's right." Cassidy gave a little laugh. "My days are all mixed-up."

Though she hadn't seen Tim since he'd left the hospital with his family on Saturday, he'd called every night to give her updates on Esther's condition. Last night, he'd put Esther on the phone and the girl had gushed how she loved, loved, loved her new pink cast.

"How are Esther and that smokin'-hot cast doing today?"

"Well, she went back to school this morning as planned," Tim informed her. "I spoke with my mother just before I stopped by your salon. She said Esther had a good day. Apparently the cast was a hit."

Cassidy smiled and wished she could hear all about Esther's first day back at school directly from her. "Tell her I said to save a place on it for me to sign. A big spot."

"You could do that this week." Tim's gaze shifted from a metal slide that glimmered in the late-afternoon sun back to Cassidy. "How 'bout we all go out for pizza?"

Though the thought was appealing, Cassidy hesitated. Since the proposal, she'd been rethinking the wisdom of spending all this time with Tim and his daughters. The last thing she wanted was to create false expectations.

"Maybe." Deliberately she kept her tone noncommittal.

They swung in silence for almost a minute when Tim cleared his throat. "Have you, ah, thought of what doctor you're going to see?"

Ah, yes, twelve weeks was right around the corner. A fact she hadn't forgotten and apparently neither had he.

"I have," Cassidy kept her tone casual. "I've got an appointment with Michelle Davis next Monday."

Michelle Davis and two other OBs had founded the "other" practice in Jackson Hole. Though it hadn't been easy to break the hold that Travis's OB group had on the area, the all-women practice was slowing carving its own niche.

Tim's swing stilled. "You weren't interested in seeing one of the doctors in my group?"

"I considered several of them." It was the truth. Cassidy had thought long and hard before making her decision. "I decided it might be awkward, with you and me involved. From everything I've heard, Michelle is a good doctor."

"She is," Tim admitted, albeit a trifle grudgingly. "I'll send her the records, so she has them for your appointment."

"Thanks."

"Speaking of the baby, I'd like to revisit our conversation from Saturday."

Cassidy had known this was coming. Tim was a focused kind of guy. When he'd shown up at her salon, she'd suspected he wasn't simply there to say hello.

He wouldn't be happy with the answer she would give him but these past few days she'd done a lot of thinking. She felt confident she was making the right decision. "Okay, let's talk."

"I had just broached the subject of marriage when we were interrupted," he said in a conversational tone.

"That certainly wasn't your fault."

"Regardless." He paused. "I wish we could have finished the discussion and arrived at a mutually agreeable resolution."

She wondered if he was aware how this sounded. Not like a marriage proposal, but like a business deal they were ready to negotiate and close.

Without waiting for her to respond, he continued, "The more I think about it, the more I realize that marriage is the answer. In fact, it's the perfect solution."

"Is it?" Cassidy kept her tone bland, her expression equally nonreactive.

Tim nodded, as if taking the comment for assent. "I've told you how I've worried that I wouldn't have enough time for a wife. But I was looking at it all wrong."

Cassidy merely lifted a brow.

His expression turned intense. "Think how convenient it would be for both of us to be under the same roof. We could split up the household and child-care duties fifty-fifty, which would take pressure off both of us. And please don't doubt for a second that I won't pull my weight."

Something in his gaze told her this was an important point, so she nodded. "I believe you."

He expelled a heavy breath and relief skittered across his face. "We would build a good life together. A happy life. What do you say?"

It was exactly what she didn't want: a business arrangement with everything split fifty-fifty. The crazy thing was, for a second Cassidy was actually tempted to say yes. Not only to erase the tension on his face but because she wanted to be with Tim. She wanted to wake up next to him every morning. She wanted to feel his arms around her when she was sad. She wanted to go to bed every night and have him beside her.

But she kept her lips pressed together and reminded herself that being married to a man who loved her, who wanted to marry her because he couldn't imagine living without her, wasn't what he was offering.

She'd spent the first eighteen years of her life feeling like an unwanted obligation. She didn't want to feel that way when she was with Tim. That would be worse than going on without him.

Stopping her slow-moving swing, Cassidy rose and reached out a hand. He stood and tugged her to him. When he wrapped his arms around her, just the comforting strength of those taut muscles beneath her fingers and the clean, fresh scent of him made her want to cry.

After a long moment, she stepped back and began to walk. He said nothing as she ignored an ornate iron bench to finally pause beneath the welcoming arms of a maple with flaming-red leaves.

Cassidy reached up and pulled a leaf from a low-hanging branch, twisting it between her fingers.

"Tell me what you're thinking," he said.

When she lifted her gaze, she saw the concern in those beautiful hazel eyes. Never had she wished so much that things could be different. That he could love her even a fraction as much as she loved him.

Love?

Cassidy could no longer deny the truth, at least to herself. Which made what she was about to say even more difficult. "I can't marry you, Tim."

"What?" A stunned look of disbelief filled his eyes. "Why not?"

"While your solution to our problem is logical—" God, she hated referring to the bun as a problem "—the truth is I won't marry anyone—not even you—because it's the convenient or responsible thing to do."

His brows slammed together. "I don't understand."

"I want the fairy tale. I want love." She gave an embarrassed laugh. "It may be stupid, but there you go. And this is probably as good of a time as any to—"

"Cassidy," he began, but having finally gathered her courage to say what must be said, she plunged ahead.

"While I know you think it's best for us to do all these things together and spend lots of time in each other's company, for right now I need you to back off."

His jaw tightened, his eyes now hooded and unreadable. "Are you saying you don't want anything more to do with me?"

"I'm saying, well, yes, I guess that is what I'm saying."

When heat flashed in his eyes and he opened his mouth, she continued on without giving him a chance to speak.

"For now," she emphasized. "Just until I can catch my breath and come to grips with everything that has happened." *Just until I can find a way to stop loving you so much.* "You're the bun's baby daddy. You'll always be a part of our life."

"Baby daddy." Tim puckered his lips as if the words were sour on his tongue. "I'll give you space, if that's what you need. But you and I both know I'm more to you than simply a baby daddy."

Without another word, he turned and strode out of the park, not once looking back.

Cassidy glanced down at the leaf now crumpled between her fingers. She opened her hand wide and watched as the breeze swept the dried and broken pieces to the ground.

Until this past week, if any man or woman had told Tim they didn't want to see him again, he'd have respected their wishes. Not this time. He feared if he did as Cassidy asked, she'd slip away from him. The thought of that was intolerable.

"Doesn't Daddy look pretty, Grandpa?" Esther commented as he stood with his daughters on the front porch of his parents' home while his mother dealt with an inside emergency brought on by that "blasted cat." Tim assumed that meant Domino had gotten into trouble...again.

"He does look pretty, sweetheart." Steve gave his son a wink. "Where are you going all spiffed up?"

The screen door of the house burst open before Tim could answer and his mother emerged, looking harried but triumphant.

"He'll never find where I hid the kitty treats." A look of smug satisfaction filled her eyes.

"Domino always finds them," Esther demurred.

"Always," Ellyn agreed from her spot on the porch swing.

"Not this time." Suzanne gave a decisive nod of her head then appeared to switch gears as her gaze settled on her son. "My, don't you look handsome, Timothy. I didn't realize you had plans for the evening."

"He's going to a wedding," Esther told her grandmother. "That's why he's wearing a suit."

"And a tie," Ellyn added.

Tim wondered if his mother would have been more or less insistent about watching the girls if she'd known he was going out. He'd initially considered turning down her plea to take care of the twins over the weekend because he didn't have any plans.

But when he'd started to say no, there'd been a flicker of something in her eyes. And the way she kept assuring him that his daughters would be safe in her care troubled him.

The last thing he wanted was for her to think he didn't trust her. After all, what had happened to Esther last weekend had been simply an accident.

"Are you going out with...Cassidy?" Suzanne asked.

Both sets of seven-year-old eyes swung to him at the sound of the familiar name. The twins had been asking him all week when they were going to see her again and it was becoming increasingly hard to come up with plausible excuses for her absence.

"Actually," Tim forced a smile, "Cassidy is working this evening."

Suzanne's brows drew together. "I don't recall anyone we know getting married. Do you, Steve?"

"You're the one who keeps track of such things," her husband told her. "Not me. I just go where I'm told."

"Who's the happy couple?" his mother pressed.

For a second, Tim went blank. Then he recalled the names. "Julie Krupicka and Dylan Lovell."

"The names don't sound familiar." His mother's face suddenly brightened. "Does Jayne know them? Will she be there?"

"No idea." Tim bent over and gave Esther a hug. Ellyn came running to get hers, too.

"We talked to Cassidy last night," Esther told her grandmother.

"You did?" Suzanne's smile froze. "How is she?"

"She misses us," Esther said.

"She's been super-duper busy," Ellyn informed her grandmother and her twin nodded.

The way Tim saw it, phoning Cassidy once a day to make sure all was well with her still constituted keeping his distance. When he'd placed the first call, the day after she'd asked him to back off, he'd worried she might not answer. But she had. He'd deliberately kept the conversation light and easy.

Last night, the girls had been in the room and insisted on speaking with her. She'd chatted with each of them longer than she had with him.

When she mentioned in passing she'd be busy working a wedding all day today, Tim considered that his invitation. Though he didn't know Julie or Dylan, he'd done a little research and discovered where the reception was being held.

*Baby daddy.*

The words continued to twist his gut.

Though he *was* the father of Cassidy's child, there was so much more between them. Tonight, he would do his darndest to make her see that this baby daddy was someone she couldn't live without.

In Cassidy's estimation, as far as brides went, Julie Krupicka was a peach, a sweet young woman not easily rattled. Like when she stepped on her train and put a gaping hole in it shortly before her walk down the aisle, she only rolled her eyes and asked if anyone had tape.

When she'd urged Cassidy and Daffodil to stay for the reception, the two women found it difficult to refuse her anything. Cassidy knew her assistant was feeling a bit blue this evening—family issues was all she'd say—and she hoped the reception would cheer Daffy up.

Right now, the petite blonde stood beside the punch bowl looking pretty in pink while visiting with a couple of clients. Cassidy had just nabbed a club soda when Dr. Noah Anson sauntered over.

Noah, a neurosurgeon, was relatively new in Jackson Hole. Thanks to the magic of her scissors, his jet-black hair looked über smash. Mr. Tall, Dark and Handsome had informed her after his first cut all those months ago that, despite her fabulous press, he'd been hesitant to get his hair cut at a place called Clippety Do Dah. Now he refused to go anywhere else.

"Dance with me?" Noah asked with an easy smile.

The band launched into a slow number and Cassidy placed her drink on a nearby table. "Only if you let me lead."

Noah laughed and whisked her onto the hardwood. Cassidy had hoped being busy would keep her mind off Tim. It hadn't worked yet, but the night was still young.

As she'd made it clear she'd be tied up all evening, tonight there would be no phone call, no teasing voice on the other end of the line asking about her day.

She should have put the kibosh on the calls when they started. But she'd been worried Esther may have had a setback. She wasn't sure what her excuse was for answering every other day this week.

"Are you and Tim still dating?"

Pulling herself from her fog, Cassidy blinked. "I'm sorry. What did you ask?"

"I asked if you and Tim Duggan are together."

Cassidy hesitated.

"We are" came a deep voice. "Mind if I cut in, Noah?"

Cassidy turned, dumbfounded to see Tim looking mouthwateringly delicious in a dark suit and red tie.

"Certainly," Noah said smoothly. He gave Cassidy a wink. "Just for fun you might want to let him lead."

Out of the corner of her eye, Cassidy saw Daffodil say something to Jewel Lucas, then scurry off as Noah left the dance floor headed in their direction.

Tim's arms closed around her and, following his lead, they were soon moving in perfect time to the lilt of a love song.

"What are you doing here?" She tipped her head back. "I didn't realize you knew Julie and Dylan."

"I don't." Tim flashed a smile. "I'm here as a personal friend of the hairstylist."

Cassidy inhaled the intoxicating scent of his cologne and for a second lost her train of thought.

"So you're saying you—" She struggled to get the words out.

"Yep. I crashed the party."

The impish gleam in his eyes brought a smile to her lips. He looked inordinately proud of his transgression.

"Why'd you do it?"

"Why else?" After a graceful dip, he spun her around. "I wanted to dance with you."

Pleasure rippled through her but she tamped it down.

"You promised to give me space." She wondered why she sounded peevish when she was so glad to see him.

"It's been four whole days since I last saw you…since I last touched you." His fingers tightened around her hand. "It feels like a lifetime."

The time apart had seemed like an eternity to her, too. But she wasn't about to admit that to him. "Where are the girls?"

"They're spending the weekend with my parents." His expression turned serious. "My mother seems to have this need to prove she can be trusted."

"What happened to Esther wasn't her fault."

"That's exactly what I told her...numerous times. I did, however, have a long talk with both girls. I made it clear the next time they want to climb a tree, they take me with them."

Despite her intention not to encourage him in any way, Cassidy laughed. Tim was a good dad. She had no doubt he'd be an equally excellent father to bun.

*If only he loved me, everything would be perfect...*

"You look tired, Cass." He brushed back a strand of her hair from her cheek.

The gentle, caring gesture nearly undid her. It was definitely time to head home. Tired and hormonal were not a good combination.

She glanced in the direction of the exit. "I believe it's time to call it a night."

"I can give you a lift home," Tim offered in an offhand tone. "If you need one."

"Thanks, but I rode with Daffy."

"Well, then, let's find her." His palm rested against the small of her back as they left the dance floor.

She supposed she could have told Tim to keep his hands to himself. But that seemed a bit overreactive so Cassidy relaxed and let herself enjoy the heat of his touch through her silk dress.

The search for Daffodil led them to every corner of the large barn where the reception was being held. After twenty minutes, Cassidy was considering calling out the dogs.

"Since she's not much of a partier, I didn't expect to find her on the dance floor." She slanted another glance around the room. "But she's also not at any of the tables or in line for a drink..."

"Jewel," Cassidy called out when she saw her friend. "Have you seen Daffodil?"

Jewel had helped with the bridal-party makeup today,

but because she lived on her grandparents' ranch—rather than in Jackson—she'd driven separately.

The pretty, dark-haired woman strolled up. She gave Tim a quizzical look. "Tim, I didn't realize you'd be here."

"Last-minute decision," he said easily.

Jewel shifted her attention back to Cassidy. "Daffy left about thirty minutes ago. She had a headache. I told her I'd take you home."

"No way. You live in the opposite direction." Cassidy waved a dismissive hand. "I'll find someone else."

"You already have someone." Tim took her hand and brought it to his mouth, planting a warm, moist kiss in the palm. "Escorting you home will be my pleasure."

## *Chapter Seventeen*

Cassidy tried to tell herself she'd never have accepted a ride from Tim if she'd known she'd end up naked. Allowing him to drive her home seemed quite innocuous. And because his house was on the way, his request to stop at his place to pick up a picture Esther and Ellyn had drawn for her seemed to make perfect sense.

When he began to kiss her just inside the front door, she had to admit she'd kissed him back. And now, lying beside him feeling like a cat that had just lapped up a whole bowl of sweet, rich cream, she couldn't even bring herself to regret her actions.

"You're so beautiful." His hand traced gentle circles on her abdomen as he nuzzled her neck.

Her lips curved up and she arched back, giving him full access to her throat. "Let's see if you're still saying that when my belly is indistinguishable from a beach ball."

"You'll be even more beautiful."

Something in the way he said the words had her believing it was true.

"I love your hair." He twined a strand around his fingers, the pale lavender shade soft in the golden glow of the lamplight. "I can't believe you ever cut it off."

They both knew he referred to that horrible time in fifth grade. She snuggled against him, the memory somehow not so disturbing when she was in his arms. Cassidy buried her face against his shoulder, inhaling the familiar scent of him, drawing strength from the closeness.

"I didn't have a choice." She spoke so softly, her words muffled against his bare flesh, that she wondered if he'd heard. Wondered if she wanted him to hear.

But his fingers stilled and he brushed his lips against her temple. When he spoke, his voice was soft and low, inviting confidences. "Will you tell me about it?"

She'd never told anyone. Not her fifth-grade teacher, the school guidance counselor or any of her friends. Her mother believed Cassidy had brought the trouble on herself.

That, Cassidy knew, was the reason she'd held the truth close all these years. Deep down she worried her mother had been right and she *had* been at fault.

"You don't have to tell me." Tim wrapped his arms even more securely around her.

Her legs remained tangled with his and her head now rested on his shoulder.

"My mother had this boyfriend." Cassidy forced the words past lips that seemed determined to hold them in. "His name was Jace."

She could see Mr. Biker-man now with his too-long blond hair pulled back in a leather tie and those pale blue eyes. Though she knew it made no sense, ever since Jace, men with blond hair had been a turn-off. "He would watch me with his creepy blue eyes, tell me I was pretty. At first I liked the attention. Then it got weird."

Tim's breath hitched but he said nothing, only stroked her back when she burrowed closer.

"Crystal giggled when she told me Jace loved my hair and thought I was sexy. *Sexy?* I was *eleven*." She swallowed hard against the sudden dryness in her throat. "When I told her he looked at me funny, she laughed and called me a tease, said if I didn't want him to notice me, I shouldn't have flirted with him."

Just remembering tied her stomach in knots. To calm herself Cassidy drew in a breath, let it out slowly. "Before Jace came over that night, I took the scissors to my hair."

His arms tightened around her. "Did it work? Did he leave you alone?"

Cassidy nodded. "Cutting it all off was worth it. By the time it grew out, Crystal was with another guy and Jace was history."

"Your mother—" Tim nearly spat the words "—should never have had a child."

"She'd agree with you on that point." Cassidy gave a humorless laugh. "Crystal told me every day that I'd ruined her life and she wished I'd never been born."

Tim tipped her face up with his fingers and gazed into her eyes. "Well, *I'm* glad you were born. And I feel honored you shared with me what happened."

Cassidy glanced down at the muscular arm wrapped around her, ran her fingers across the soft hair dusting his forearm. "I think the reason I kept it to myself all these years was because I was afraid whoever I told would blame me."

"For what?" he asked, sounding genuinely perplexed.

She lifted her gaze, met those warm hazel eyes. "I liked it—at first—when he told me I was pretty."

"Oh, honey, most girls like to be told they're pretty. But

you were a child. He was a man." His jaw set in a tight line and she could see him fight for composure. "None of it was your fault."

Cassidy exhaled a ragged breath and a couple of tears slipped down her cheeks.

"Tonight doesn't change anything," she muttered, swiping the tears away. The closeness, the trust, meant nothing. Not without love.

"Close your eyes," Tim whispered.

"Did you hear me?" She yawned, exhausted. "It doesn't change—"

"I heard you." He tugged the sheet over her and watched as she slept, the crescents of her lashes dark against her ivory skin.

She was wrong. Tonight had changed everything.

There was a connection between them, a strong one, arising from trust and love.

*Love?*

Tim rolled the word around on his tongue. Smiled at the rightness of it.

"I love you," he whispered to the sleeping woman beside him. "And I won't lose you."

Cassidy woke to the enticing aroma of freshly brewed coffee and… She rolled over, sniffed the air and smiled.

Although last night felt like a dream, the scent of sizzling bacon and the rumpled sheets tangled around her told her it had all been real.

Pushing to a sitting position, Cassidy cast aside the covers remembering how Tim had reached for her again during the night, after only a couple hours of sleep. The fire that burned between them could not be quenched. Even now, a hot riff of need shivered up her spine. She wondered if he'd be interested in another encore this morning.

Her earlier resolve to keep him at arm's length now

seemed naive, foolish and totally unnecessary. She liked being with Tim, enjoyed his company and craved his touch. Why shouldn't she go out with him occasionally and sleep with him when the opportunity arose?

It didn't have to be all or nothing. After all, she would be raising his child, so they would be forever connected. Though she knew adoption was a wonderful option for many, once she felt the baby move, there had been only one choice for her. She would take classes, ask for advice and do her best to be a good mother.

Cassidy rose, feeling more encouraged about the future than she'd been in weeks. She glanced around for something to wear besides last night's silk dress.

The dress wasn't a favorite and the thought of putting it on rubbed like a too-tightly bristled brush. Cassidy wandered over to Tim's dresser.

Precisely folded stacks of cotton shirts sat in the first drawer she opened. She chose a long-sleeved one the color of freshly mown grass, tugging the soft garment over her head and pushing up the sleeves. The lower edge barely covered her bottom but she had a feeling Tim wouldn't mind.

Now that she was more or less fully dressed, she glanced in the mirror. Fully prepared for disaster, she saw nothing a little lip color couldn't handle. Relieved, she raked a hand through the tangles in her hair. After a quick pit stop in the master bathroom, Cassidy headed downstairs with Ravish Me Red on her lips and a spring in her step.

As she approached the kitchen, she heard Tim whistling slightly off-key, his back to her as he scrambled eggs.

Her heart flip-flopped.

Like a predatory cat, Cassidy moved across the tile floor. She slipped her arms around his waist and placed her lips against his ear. "Guess who?"

She felt his face crease into a smile before he moved the skillet to an empty burner, cut the heat and turned. "Why, it's just who I wanted to see this morning."

He held her at arm's length. His gaze traveled down then back up, darkening at the large expanse of leg displayed. Though his hair was still slightly damp from the shower, he was fully dressed, ready for whatever the day had to offer.

Cassidy began to unbutton his shirt. "You have way too many clothes on."

He glanced at the eggs. "I made breakfa—"

"Eggs can wait." Cassidy slid her hands up his chest then leaned forward and planted a kiss against his throat. "We're alone. It would be practically criminal not to take advantage of the opportunity."

"I like the way you think." He cupped her bottom. "In fact, I like everything about you."

Sex talk, she told herself. Still, the words sent a warm rush of pleasure coursing through her veins. "Flattery will get you under my, er, your, shirt."

Pushing that shirt upward, heat sparked in his eyes when he discovered she didn't have anything on underneath. He grinned. "This is convenient."

They were the last words spoken for a long while. Cassidy had never made love in a kitchen before but she quickly discovered Tim had a talent for figuring out new uses for chairs and tables.

They finished in the shower and by the time they got out, she was starving. After pulling on the badly wrinkled dress, she reached for her panties.

Sitting on the bed, back in jeans and a different Henley, Tim made a sound of displeasure.

Cassidy smiled to herself and turned. "I'm afraid the bun needs to eat."

To her surprise, instead of a joking retort or a grabbing reach, Tim's eyes took on a soft glow. "I love you, Cassidy."

"Luv ya, too, babe."

"I'm serious."

Hope leaped in her breast but she ruthlessly shoved it down and forced a light tone. "That's what every guy says when he's just had the best sex of his life."

Turning from his scrutinizing gaze, Cassidy busied herself smoothing wrinkles from her dress.

But Tim refused to be pushed aside so easily. He grasped her hand and tugged her close. "This isn't about sex, Cassidy. This is about you. I love you. I want to marry you."

Her heart plummeted. It didn't take a rocket scientist to put these puzzle pieces together. Tim was a decisive guy. When faced with an issue, he thought and studied then went after what he wanted with methodical precision.

He'd made it clear he wanted them to be married by the time the baby was born. She'd made it clear the only reason she'd marry was for love. It was obvious he'd decided the easiest way to get what he wanted was to simply tell her what she needed to hear.

Disappointment flooded her. She'd expected better of him. Marshalling her emotions, she met his gaze. "Don't lie to me."

A look of startled surprise crossed his face. "I wouldn't lie about something this important. I love you, Cass."

There was sincerity in his voice and in the penetrating gaze he fixed on her. Still, this seemed awfully damned convenient.

"I don't know that I believe you." God, she wanted to believe him, but if she did and then found out he'd lied…

She closed her eyes against the stabbing pain.

His arms tightened around her and his voice took on urgency. "How can I convince you I'm sincere?"

She rested her head against his forehead and sighed. "I don't know, Tim. I don't know."

\* \* \*

When Hailey Ferris stopped by the salon on Monday to ask if she had time to grab a coffee, Cassidy pulled her into the back office and shut the door.

"What's up, Cass?" The pretty blonde asked, looking more intrigued than startled by the manhandling.

"Tim stopped by my apartment this morning," she told her friend. "With a caramel macchiato."

It was clear to Cassidy that Tim wasn't going to give up his pursuit. What had been equally clear to her was she didn't want him to stop.

"Do you think he'd stop by my house? Nonfat peppermint mocha with whipped cream and chocolate shavings."

Cassidy ignored the comment. "This situation is serious."

Hailey instantly sobered. "Tell me."

Once she started talking, Cassidy couldn't seem to stop. She didn't leave anything out. No detail was too small to share with Hailey.

"The love stuff was just crazy talk after mind-blowing sex, right?" Cassidy asked.

"I never thought of using a kitchen chair in that way." Hailey returned to a detail she appeared to find particularly intriguing. "I think Winn and I are going to have to give that a try tonight when Cam is at ball practice."

"This isn't about the kitchen chair." Cassidy swatted at Hailey's arm in exasperation, then had to grin. Just revisiting that night—and the following morning—gave her a pleasurable jolt. "Though it all was pretty fantastic."

Hailey's blue eyes twinkled. "You two were obviously on fire."

Cassidy's smile faded. "We were. But I can't marry someone just because I like him and the sex is fantastic."

"*And* he's your baby daddy," Hailey pointed out. Her friend had been upset at first that she hadn't been told before about "bun" but accepted Cassidy's reasoning for keeping the pregnancy quiet.

"The baby is why he's doing it, Hailey." Cassidy huffed out a breath. "That's the only reason he's hanging with me now, because he's determined to do the honorable thing and marry me."

Hailey's gaze turned thoughtful. "Doesn't sound like you think much of yourself."

Cassidy bristled at the hint of censure underlying her friend's words. "What are you saying?"

"You're a beautiful, sexy, successful woman. You bring light into everyone's life. Why wouldn't Tim fall in love with you?" A devilish gleam lit Hailey's eyes. "Don't forget, you're great in the kitchen."

## Chapter Eighteen

On Tuesday, when Tim found himself with a break between morning surgery and afternoon clinic, he headed to Hill of Beans for a quick lunch.

The fact that Cassidy's salon was just down the street hadn't escaped his notice. On his way back to the clinic, he would pick up a bouquet of daisies, then head over to Clippety Do Dah to deliver them in person.

Yesterday, he'd stopped by her apartment on his way to the hospital and dropped off her favorite drink, a caramel macchiato. As he'd handed her the beverage, he'd indulged in his favorite morning pick-me-up, a kiss from the woman he loved.

Still smiling at the thought of the kiss, he pushed open the door to Hill of Beans. Bells jingled and Cole Lassiter looked up from behind the counter and lifted a hand in greeting. When Cole had returned to Jackson Hole and decided to run his coffee-shop empire from his hometown, Tim had been as surprised as anyone.

"Hey, Doogie," Cole said.

Tim winced. "Hey, Lassister, looking good in that barista apron."

"Meg finds it sexy," Cole said, referring to his wife, who happened to be the sister of Travis Fisher, Tim's colleague.

"Better be careful," Tim joked. "Or you'll find yourself with another baby on the way."

"That'd be okay with us. We want a whole houseful." Cole shot Tim a curious glance. "I hear you and my good buddy Cassidy Kaye are seeing each other."

Though it was a comment, there was a definite question in there somewhere. Believing it was up to Cassidy to decide how much to tell her friends, Tim deflected.

"I didn't realize you and Cassidy were good friends," Tim said after giving Cole his order.

While there was still much about Cassidy he didn't know, Tim reassured himself he'd have a lifetime to discover everything about the woman he loved.

"Cass and I grew up together. She's like my kid sister." Warmth filled Cole's eyes. "She, Keenan and I were tight. Strength in the midst of adversity you might say. It's difficult to know which of us had it worse."

"She told me about her mother."

Cole's face registered surprise as he expertly made Tim's turkey sandwich on wheat. "You two must be closer than I thought. Cass rarely talks about Crystal."

Tim lifted a shoulder in a slight shrug.

"Cassidy stopped to pick up a scone this morning." A frown pulled at Cole's dark brows. "She didn't look good."

Tim instantly went on alert. "What do you mean?"

"She wasn't her normal chipper self." The lines between Cole's brows deepened. "When I asked, she said she had a bad headache."

As Cole handed him the sandwich and a bottle of water, Tim added a large coffee to the order. If Cassidy was sick…

Well, if she was sick, he was a doctor. And he would darn well take care of her, whether she wanted him to or not.

This time, she wouldn't push him away.

When the headache first began, Cassidy had thought she'd simply been thinking too hard about her situation with Tim. Eventually she'd concluded her old friend Mr. Migraine had come to visit and decided to stay for a while.

The pounding in Cassidy's head now beat like a hammer behind her right eye.

Over the past hour the throbbing had escalated, becoming a tangible thing, driving away all thoughts. All she knew was pain. Keeping her eyes shut, she tried to block out everything. She wished she'd thought to turn the blinds to keep out the sun.

"Cassidy, sweetheart. Can you tell me what's wrong?"

She opened her eyes—just a slit—to find Tim kneeling beside the sofa, his brow furrowed and his eyes filled with concern.

"Other than the sadistic troll pounding my right eye with a hammer?" She shut her lids tight and winced. "How'd you get in?"

"The key under the mat." He gave a low chuckle. "For once you locked the door."

"What are you doing here?"

"Checking on you." His fingers were cool and gentle against her forehead. "Have you had migraines before?"

"Yes," she admitted. "But not recently."

"Any other symptoms besides the pounding behind your right eye?"

"Some nausea," she murmured. "And the troll goes nuts when I move."

As if to illustrate, she shifted her head slightly then whimpered.

"Have you taken anything?"

Cassidy kept her eyes closed and remained perfectly still. "I was afraid to take anything. Because of the baby…"

"I'll get you some Tylenol," he said. "Cole told me you had a headache, so I brought coffee. Extra shot of espresso. The caffeine should help."

"Could you shut the blinds?" she asked when he rose to get the Tylenol.

"Absolutely."

She could hear him talking to someone in the kitchen but couldn't make out the words.

He helped her sit up and she swallowed the pills with a couple gulps of water. Then he handed her the coffee.

Caffeine had helped in the past, but she hadn't had the energy to make a cup for herself. She sipped as the troll continued his hammering.

"Who were you speaking with? In the kitchen?"

"Travis." He smiled slightly but the worry remained in his eyes. "He's going to take my patients this afternoon."

She started to shake her head then winced.

"I'm not leaving, so don't bother telling me to go."

Cassidy took another sip of coffee. "I don't have the energy to argue."

"Good." Tim squeezed her hand. "I'm going to get you a cool compress for your head."

After another concerned look, he disappeared. Seconds later Tim returned. He placed a moist washcloth on her forehead then took a seat on the sofa beside her. "Lean back against me."

Cassidy didn't have the energy to refuse. She wasn't sure how much time had passed, but by the time she finished the coffee and placed the empty cup on the trunk, she felt almost human.

"Better?"

"A lot." She tried a smile. "I think the troll is taking a break. I hope he doesn't come back."

His eyes searched her face in the dim light. "There's one other thing that might help. Put your head in my lap."

"Why?"

"You must be feeling better." He motioned her closer. "Massage often helps with migraines. When my mother used to get them—"

He stopped abruptly as if fearing any mention of Suzanne might cause the troll to start swinging again. "Just trust me."

Once her head rested in his lap, his fingers delved through the loose strands to her scalp and stroked tenderly.

"That feels wonderful," she murmured.

"Shh. Just close your eyes and relax."

Cassidy wasn't sure when she drifted off or how long she slept. When she awoke she was still on the sofa, only her head rested on a purple throw pillow. Tim, instead of sitting up, was stretched out beside her.

When she stirred, he shifted and pushed to one elbow. "How do you feel?"

"What time is it?"

His gaze scanned her face. "My question first."

She knew she must look horrible. She hadn't put on lipstick all day. Then she realized she must be feeling better if she was thinking about her appearance.

"How do you feel?" Tim repeated.

She moved her head slowly from side to side. "Troll and hammer vanquished."

His smile flashed. "Hungry?"

As if in answer, her stomach growled.

"Let me see what I can rustle up."

"What about the girls?" She slowly pushed herself to a sitting position. "Don't you need to pick them up?"

"Lindsey and Zach are taking them to an exhibit at the wildlife museum tonight."

"Had that been on the agenda?"

"New plans," he said.

"Does your mother know where you are? Or rather who you're with?"

Tim's expression didn't change. "My mother is aware how I feel about you. I've made it clear I won't tolerate her interference."

She met his gaze, her chin lifted in a stubborn tilt. "I won't come between you and your mother."

"Don't worry." He reached over and took her hand, his thumb drawing little circles on the palm. "Once she sees how happy we are together, she'll come around."

She averted her gaze. "Did you say something about food?"

"I love you, Cassidy. I want to marry you."

Cassidy thought of the men she'd dated. One, who'd come from a prominent ranching family, had pledged his undying love. In the end, that love hadn't been strong enough to weather his parents' disapproval of a hairdresser with a junkie mother.

Tim was close to his family. For a relationship to work between them, Suzanne would have to accept her.

Despite Tim's optimism, Cassidy knew that would be a cold day in hell.


"I need your help in planning a party for this Friday," Tim told his mother as they sat on the porch swing while his father played ball with the twins in the front yard.

"That's not much notice, but I can pull it together." Suzanne's heart lifted. She'd been worried she may have caused irreparable harm to her relationship with her son, but having him ask for her help said they were back on solid ground. "What kind of party?"

His gaze met hers. "An engagement party."

Puzzled, Suzanne inclined her head. She thought of Tim's friends but couldn't think of one who might be getting married soon. "Who is this for?"

"For me," he said. "I'm going to ask Cassidy to marry me. I pray she says yes."

Despite feeling as if she'd been whacked in the chest with a sledgehammer, Suzanne kept her surging emotions under tight control. She should have seen this coming. The woman was carrying Tim's baby. Her grandchild.

Odd, how she'd never thought of it that way.

"Of course she'll accept," Suzanne said, seizing on a point where they could both agree.

"I'm not so sure. She doesn't believe I love her," he said. "Even though I do. Very much."

Suzanne said nothing, surprised by the intensity of emotion in her son's voice.

"We're a perfect match," he added.

Reminding herself she'd already lost one child and couldn't afford to alienate her son, Suzanne kept her voice conversational. "Is that right?"

"She's smart and funny and kind and great with the girls. We both like outdoor sports and share a passion for horror flicks." Tim's lips curved up in a smile. "She's the most upbeat person I know. She brings joy into my life. I can be too serious."

Suzanne almost argued the point then reluctantly admitted it was a correct assessment. She realized something else, too.

"You *have* seemed happier since you and Cassidy got together," she reluctantly conceded.

"Cass doesn't sweat the small stuff and she's easygoing." His expression grew determined. "But that doesn't mean I'm going to take advantage of her generous spirit. I want her to be happy, too. Whatever compromises I need to make, I'll make them."

This was a side to Tim that Suzanne hadn't seen before, not even with Caro. Why had she been so unwilling to accept the woman as a potential mate for her son?

Because her hair was a different color every time she saw her?

Because she dressed differently than most of the women Suzanne knew?

Remembering the things she'd said to Cassidy after the "color party" brought a wash of shame to Suzanne's cheeks. The young woman probably hated her. Suzanne couldn't blame her.

"She doesn't want to come between us," Tim went on to explain. "That's why I thought if she knew you'd helped with the party—"

"She told you she didn't want to come between us?"

"I assured her you'd come around, that when you realized how happy she made me, you'd be glad she was in my life."

"Get up," Suzanne ordered.

Tim's eyes widened. "What?"

"Get up. If we're going to pull this party together in less than three days, we need to get started."

"You're really going to help me?"

The look of startled disbelief on his face made her smile.

"There's nothing I like more than happy endings." Suzanne patted his cheek. "Especially when it involves someone I love."

## Chapter Nineteen

"I can't believe your mother rented out Wally's Place for your dad's birthday." Cassidy glanced over at Tim as they strolled down the sidewalk toward the popular bar. "That must have cost a fortune."

"I'm not sure how much it cost." All Tim knew was when he'd mentioned that he'd like to propose to Cassidy in Wally's where they'd had their first date, his mother had suggested they might as well have the party there… and then insisted on paying for everything.

"How old is your dad today?"

"Ah, sixty-two." Or, Tim thought, he would be, next month.

"I feel like a schmuck not bringing a gift," Cassidy said with a slight frown. "I may not be an etiquette queen but it seems a person should bring a present to a birthday party."

His fingers tightened around her hand as his heart galloped in his chest. He tried to tell himself it wasn't the end of the world if she turned him down tonight. He would simply soldier on until he convinced her that his feelings were real.

"Tim, did you hear me? Your dad will expect a gift."

"Give him one next month."

"Why would I do that?"

"You're right. That makes no sense." Tim forced a laugh then redirected the conversation. "You look lovely tonight."

Cassidy's quick smile of pleasure had him wanting to kiss her and propose right then and there.

"I wasn't sure what to wear," she told him, looking quite serious. "I've never been to a birthday party for someone's dad. But then, it is at Wally's Place."

She reminded him of a fairy princess in her white tulle skirt with an enormous pink bow tied around her waist and pink cowboy boots. The blue denim shirt added her unique brand to the outfit.

"The girls are going to be blown away when they see you," Tim said in admiration. "We're going to have to go out and buy them boots and skirts to match."

"I wish they could have ridden with us." Two lines formed between Cassidy's brows. "It seems like forever since I've seen Esther and Ellyn."

"My mother thought it'd be nice for us to have some time alone." Tim nearly groaned aloud. He couldn't believe he'd brought up his *mother*. The last thing he wanted was to darken Cassidy's mood.

When they reached Wally's, he pushed open the saloon-like doors then stepped aside to let Cassidy enter. She'd barely set both feet onto the rough floorboards when she inhaled sharply and gaped. "It's—it's gorgeous."

The rugged cowboy bar known for its no-nonsense atmosphere and decor—including peanut shells on the floor—was awash in color. Streamers of purple tulle had been strung from rugged beams. Tables with glittering emerald tablecloths had been topped with centerpieces of purple hydrangeas. White lights gave the bar a festive flair.

"Tim. Cassidy." Suzanne hurried up, casually chic in black pants with heels and a lacy white shirt.

After giving her son a hug, she turned to Cassidy and gave her one as well.

"I'm so happy you're both here."

Cassidy eyed Tim's mother warily. Though she didn't smell alcohol on Suzanne's breath, the woman was definitely acting strangely.

Suzanne stepped back and took Cassidy's arm, then shifted her attention to Tim. "I was wondering if I could speak with Cassidy privately. I promise not to keep her long."

Beside her, Tim stiffened. "I don't think that's a good idea."

"Tim." Suzanne's voice was low and filled with an emotion Cassidy couldn't identify. "Please."

Tim glanced at Cassidy.

She lifted a shoulder in a slight shrug.

"Okay," he said reluctantly, giving Cassidy's hand a squeeze before he released her. "Don't keep her long."

"Thank you." Suzanne exhaled, almost as if she'd been holding her breath. She smiled brightly at Cassidy. "Let's step over here, if you don't mind."

The last thing Cassidy wanted was a private conversation with Suzanne, but at this point it didn't appear she had much choice.

"What's on your mind?" she asked when Suzanne pulled her aside.

"An apology." The woman's lips trembled slightly before she brought them under control. "I've been horrid to you. The things I've said are inexcusable."

Cassidy remained silent, not sure how to respond. Was

this some sort of joke? But the tears in Suzanne's eyes appeared very real.

"Why the change of heart?" Cassidy gestured to her outfit. "Nothing has changed with me. I'm still white trash."

Tim's mother flinched as if she'd been slapped. But she quickly recovered.

"You are not and never have been anything but an intelligent, successful woman who came from nothing and has made something of herself." Suzanne met Cassidy's gaze. "Yes, you march to the beat of your own drummer. What's wrong with that? The world would be a boring place if we were all the same."

Cassidy's heart swelled but she fought hard to contain the emotion. "Did Tim put you up to this?"

"My son made it clear to me that he loves you," Suzanne said simply. "In listening to him extol your virtues, seeing how happy he is with you, well, it made me realize I've been wrong about so many things. There is no excuse for how I acted, for all the horrid things I said. But I'd appreciate it very much if you could find it in your heart to forgive me and we could start fresh."

Silence filled the air between them for one heartbeat, then two.

"Ah, sure," Cassidy said finally. The halfhearted acceptance was the best she could muster at the moment.

"Thank you." Suzanne squeezed her arm, blinking rapidly. She cleared her throat. "I'll be calling this week to set up a time for you and me and the twins to have one of those color parties they can't quit talking about."

Cassidy simply nodded. She wondered just when she'd stepped into the alternate universe, a strange world inhabited by Suzanne-the-Sweetie-Pie.

"Time's up." Tim appeared at her side and took her arm. "Cassidy and I have important business."

It was an odd excuse to extricate her from his mother's

clutches but Cassidy was grateful he'd pulled her away before Suzanne insisted on a group hug. The way the woman was acting, that was a distinct possibility.

"Your mother is acting very strange," she said when they were out of earshot.

Tim stiffened. "Why? What did she say?"

Cassidy wasn't sure how to properly convey what had just occurred. "Long story short—she wants us to be friends."

"What do you think about that possibility?" He spoke slowly as if carefully choosing each word.

Cassidy thought for a moment. "Better than having her as an enemy."

Tim exhaled an audible breath. "I believe in time the two of you will be good friends."

She rolled her eyes but doubted Tim saw the gesture. He was too busy maneuvering them through the crowd, past good friends, without stopping.

"Your father seems to know most of the people we do," she observed. "Where are we going? And why are you in such a hurry?"

He finally stopped beside the mechanical bull.

Suddenly she understood. The bull was available and he wanted to ensure they got a ride before there was a line. "You want to go first? Or can I?"

In answer, he put his arms on her waist and sat her up on the bull. When she started to swing a leg over, he stopped her. "Just give me a minute. There's something I need to say."

"Wow. This seems to be a night for conversations." Despite her teasing words, she smiled encouragingly then frowned when she saw the perspiration dotting his brow. "Is something wrong?"

"No." He took her hand, kissed her fingers. "Everything is absolutely right."

She blinked as he dropped to one knee before her and pulled out a sparkly emerald-cut yellow diamond.

"When I was trying to think of the perfect place to formally propose, this came to mind. Although it's not a conventional location, our relationship isn't conventional, so it seemed perfect." His gaze met hers. "It was here, on our very first date, that I realized you were truly someone special."

"I—" Cassidy opened her mouth then closed it.

He caressed the top of her hand with his thumb. "I didn't think I was ready for a relationship, but being with you made me realize that I'd been living my life on an even keel. It was pleasant, comfortable. But once you came into my life, it was no longer enough."

Cassidy forced herself to breathe, her gaze riveted to his face.

"While I never expected to fall in love again, that's exactly what happened. I want to marry you, Cassidy. I want to raise children with you, to grow old with you. Though love wasn't in my plans, I'm glad it happened. I'm glad *you* happened. I can't imagine my life without you in it."

The emotion she'd been trying so hard to contain swamped her. Tears slipped down her cheeks.

"Will you do me the honor of becoming my wife? Will you be a mother to Esther and Ellyn and any other children we will have?"

The love was there in his eyes, so clear she wondered how she'd missed seeing it before. Had Hailey been right? Had she simply not felt worthy? It scarcely mattered now.

Cassidy took a deep breath. "I love you, Tim. And Esther and Ellyn and our baby, too. I can't imagine anything better than going through life with someone I love who loves me. So yes, I will marry you. Yes, yes, yes."

No longer able to contain herself, Cassidy flung herself forward into his arms, sending them both sprawling, laughing as they rolled back on the cushioned mat.

Before she could sit up, Tim slipped the ring on her finger and kissed her soundly.

"She said yes," someone, who sounded an awful lot like Suzanne, called out in a joyous voice.

Applause filled the saloon and a second later the girls joined them. For an instant, Cassidy expected Domino to appear and jump into the fray. That was just how wonderfully crazy the moment felt.

Even when they were back on their feet, accepting congratulations, Tim kept her close. Standing there beside the man she loved, surrounded by friends and family, Cassidy knew there was nowhere else she would rather be. Not only for now, but for eternity.

## *Epilogue*

Last week when her due date had come—and gone—Cassidy had waited a few days then declared the "bun" had cooked long enough and was ready to come out of the oven. But it seemed her pregnant-mama intuition wasn't considered a good enough reason for her doctor to induce. Tim said nothing, probably knowing this wasn't an argument he could win. Her mother-in-law, however, sympathized.

Suzanne had stopped over today with another gift for the baby. Cassidy suspected Tim had asked his mother to check in on her. She'd worked until her due date, expecting she'd soon have a baby to keep her busy. But the bun was still cooking and with the twins in school and Tim at the hospital, Cassidy was going stir-crazy.

"These bright colors will work whether you have a boy or girl." Suzanne added a bright purple, gold and blue plush elephant to the mountain of other stuffed creatures decorating the colorful nursery.

"Esi and Elle are convinced they're getting a sister." Cassidy brought a hand to her back, hoping to still the ache. "Tim thinks the baby is a boy."

"I can't wait to meet my new grandchild." Suzanne hesitated. "Would you…would you like some help after you come home with the baby? I understand if you prefer not—"

"I'd love it." Cassidy breathed a sigh of relief. This baby was a first for her. Despite the parenting classes she and Tim had attended, she didn't feel at all confident in her ability to care for a tiny being smaller than Domino.

Speaking of the cat…

"Have you seen Dom?"

"Out of my sight is just how I like him." Suzanne swiped a dismissive hand in the air. "When you and Tim said you wanted to give the cat to the girls as a wedding present, I wanted to kiss you both."

"The twins adore him." Cassidy smiled. "Tim and I like him well enough."

"Meow."

Cassidy glanced around and finally spotted the fat black-and-white cat perched on top of the open nursery door. "There he is."

Suzanne rolled her eyes and patted Cassidy's arm. "Once again, thank you."

Cassidy laughed. Ever since the engagement party— she'd discovered Tim's father wouldn't have a birthday for another month—her relationship with Suzanne had been on the upswing.

Though the woman was still bossy at times, Cassidy found she rather enjoyed Suzanne's outspokenness. And somehow, in the five months since Cassidy and Tim had married, Suzanne had become the mother she'd never had.

A pain ripped through her midsection, nearly bringing

Cassidy to her knees. She gasped and reached out, steadying herself against the crib.

Suzanne whirled, then immediately hurried to her daughter-in-law's side. With gentle hands she helped Cassidy to the nearby rocking chair.

"It hurts." Cassidy squeezed her eyes shut. "So much."

Whining was such an unattractive quality but this time it couldn't be helped.

She tried to focus on the breathing techniques she'd learned but couldn't concentrate. The pain seemed to ebb only to build again seconds later.

Suzanne crouched down, took her hand. "When did the pains start?"

"I've been having them all day," Cassidy admitted then gasped as another contraction squeezed like a vise. "In the past couple of hours they've become more frequent."

"Why didn't you tell me?"

"I didn't want to ruin the afternoon."

"Oh, honey." Suzanne placed a cool hand against her cheek. "We're family."

Cassidy gasped again, her hand moving to her belly as her body arched back.

"Breathe." Suzanne smoothed Cassidy's hair back from her face. "You're doing fine."

"Cass. Mom. Where are you?"

Relief spurted through Cassidy. Tim had promised to come home for lunch but she'd forgotten.

"Get up here," Suzanne called out in a voice that would have done a drill sergeant proud.

In seconds, Tim was crouched beside Cassidy, his coat unbuttoned, his hair windblown, his gaze sharp and assessing.

"Your wife is in labor," Suzanne advised, as if she was the obstetrician, not him. "The contractions are on top of each other."

"Looks like you were right, sweetheart. You said the bun was ready to make an appearance." Tim spoke in a soothing tone, one hand on her belly, his wrist cocked so he could see his watch.

"That was two weeks ago." Cassidy panted. Discomfort? Bull. This was agony.

Within minutes Tim told her it looked as if their child had decided to be born at home. Once he and his mother helped Cassidy to the bedroom, Tim checked her progress.

He looked up. Grinned. "We've got ourselves a redhead, Cass."

"You can see the hair?" Suzanne asked from her position beside Cassidy.

"The bun is ready to pop out of the oven," Tim said with a wink, then told Cassidy it was time to push.

Suzanne held her hand, murmuring words of reassurance.

Fifteen minutes later, the bun arrived perfectly cooked and ready to greet the world. Declan Timothy Duggan was an eight-pound, fourteen-ounce boy with an amazing amount of red hair and stellar lungs.

Tim pronounced his son absolutely perfect. When he laid Declan in Cassidy's arms, the baby quieted immediately.

"He's beautiful." Tears filled Suzanne's eyes as she gazed at her latest grandchild. "I'm going to make tea, call your father and give him the good news."

She was almost to the door when Cassidy called out her name.

"Thank you," Cassidy said when she turned. "I couldn't have done it without you."

Suzanne met Cassidy's gaze. "Declan and the girls are lucky to have you for their mother."

Cassidy swallowed past the lump in her throat. From Suzanne there was no higher praise. She dropped her gaze back to the baby at her breast and her heart overflowed with love.

Tim sat down on the bed beside her and trailed a gentle finger down his son's cheek. He smiled at his wife. "Did you ever think a bachelor auction would lead to all this?"

"Of course," she told him. "Why do you think I didn't let Leila get the winning bid?"

Tim was still laughing when he kissed her.

\* \* \* \* \*

THIS WAS HER favorite kind of Haven Point evening.

McKenzie Shaw locked the front door of her shop, Point Made Flowers and Gifts. The day had been long and hectic, filled with customers and orders, which was wonderful, but also plenty of unavoidable mayoral business.

She was tired and wanted to stretch out on the terrace or her beloved swing, with her feet up and something cool at her elbow. The image beckoned but the sweetness of the view in front of her made her pause.

"Hold on," she said to Paprika, her cinnamon standard poodle. The dog gave her a long-suffering look but settled next to the bench in front of the store.

McKenzie sat and reached a hand down to pet Rika's curly hair. A few sailboats cut through the stunning blue waters of Lake Haven, silvery and bright in the fading light, with the rugged, snowcapped mountains as a backdrop.

She didn't stop nearly often enough to soak in the beautiful view or enjoy the June evening air, tart and clean from the mighty fir and pines growing in abundance around the lake.

A tourist couple walked past holding hands and eating gelato cones from Carmela's, their hair backlit into golden halos by the setting sun. From a short distance away, she could hear children laughing and shrieking as they played on the beach at the city park and the alluring scent of grilling steak somewhere close by made her stomach grumble.

She loved every season here on the lake but the magnificent Haven Point summers were her favorite—especially lazy summer evenings filled with long shadows and spectacular sunsets.

Kayaking on the lake, watching children swim out to the floating docks, seeing old-timers in ancient boats casting gossamer lines out across the water. It was all part of the magic of Haven Point's short summer season.

The town heavily depended on the influx of tourists during the summer, though it didn't come close to the crowds enjoyed by their larger city to the north, Shelter Springs—especially since the Haven Point Inn burned down just before Christmas and had yet to be rebuilt.

Shelter Springs had more available lodging, more restaurants, more shopping—as well as more problems with parking, traffic congestion and crime, she reminded herself.

"Evening, Mayor," Mike Bailey called, waving as he rumbled past the store in the gorgeous old blue '57 Chevy pickup he'd restored.

She waved back, then nodded to Luis Ayala, locking up his insurance agency across the street.

A soft, warm feeling of contentment seeped through her. This was her town, these were her people. She was part of it, just like the Redemption Mountains across the lake. She had fought to earn that sense of belonging since the day she showed up, a lost, grieving, bewildered girl.

She had worked hard to earn the respect of her friends and neighbors. The chance to serve as the mayor had never been something she sought but she had accepted the challenge willingly. It wasn't about power or influence—not that one could find much of either in a small town like Haven Point. She simply wanted to do anything she could to make a difference in her community. She wanted to think she was serving with honor and dignity, but she was fully aware there were plenty in town who might disagree.

Her stomach growled, louder this time. That steak smelled as if it was charred to perfection. Too bad she didn't know who was grilling it or she might just stop by to say hello. McKenzie was briefly tempted to stop in at Serrano's or even grab a gelato of her own at Carmela's—stracciatella, her particular favorite—but she decided she would be better off taking Rika home.

"Come on, girl. Let's go."

The dog jumped to her feet, all eager, lanky grace, and McKenzie gripped the leash and headed off.

She lived not quite a mile from her shop downtown and she and Rika both looked forward all day to this evening walk along the trail that circled the lake.

As she walked, she waved at people walking, biking, driving, even boating past when the shoreline came into view. It was quite a workout for her arm but she didn't mind. Each wave was another reminder that this was her town and she loved it.

"Let's grill some chicken when we get home," she said aloud to Rika, whose tongue lolled out with appropriate enthusiasm.

Talking to her dog again. Not a good sign but she decided it was too beautiful an evening to worry about her decided lack of any social life to speak of. Town council meetings absolutely didn't count.

When she reached her lakeside house, however, she discovered a luxury SUV with California plates in the driveway of the house next to hers, with boat trailer and gleaming wooden boat attached.

Great.

Apparently someone had rented the Sloane house.

Normally she would be excited about new neighbors but in this case, she knew the tenants would only be temporary. Since moving to Shelter Springs, Carole Sloane-Hall had been renting out the house she received as a settlement in her divorce for a furnished vacation rental. Sometimes people stayed for a week or two, sometimes only a few days.

It was a lovely home, probably one of the most luxurious lakefront rentals within the city limits. Though not large, it had huge windows overlooking the lake, a wide flagstone terrace and a semiprivate boat dock—which, unfortunately, was shared between McKenzie's own property and Carole's rental house.

She wouldn't let it spoil her evening, she told herself. Usually the renters were very nice people, quiet and polite. She generally tried to act as friendly and welcoming as possible.

It wouldn't bother her at all except the two properties had virtually an open backyard because both needed access to the shared dock, with only some landscaping between the houses that ended several yards from the high watermark. Sometimes she found the lack of privacy a little disconcerting, with strangers temporarily living next door, but Carole assured her she planned to put the house on the market at the end of the summer. With everything else McKenzie had to worry about, she had relegated the vacation rental situation next door to a distant corner of her brain.

New neighbors or not, though, she still adored her own house. She had purchased it two years earlier and still felt a little rush of excitement when she unlocked the front door and walked over the threshold.

Over those two years, she had worked hard to make it her own, sprucing it up with new paint, taking down a few walls and adding one in a better spot. The biggest expense had been for the renovated master bath, which now contained a huge claw-foot tub, and the new kitchen with warm travertine countertops and the intricately tiled backsplash she had done herself.

This was hers and she loved every inch of it, almost more than she loved her little store downtown.

She walked through to the back door and let Rika off her leash. Though the yard was only fenced on one side, just as the Sloane house was fenced on the corresponding outer property edge, Rika was well trained and never left the yard.

Her cell phone rang as she was throwing together a quick lemon-tarragon marinade for the chicken.

Some days, she wanted to grab her kayak, paddle out to the middle of Lake Haven—where it was rumored to be so deep, the bottom had never been truly charted—and toss the stupid thing overboard.

This time when she saw the caller ID, she smiled, wiped her hands on a dish towel and quickly answered. "Hey, Devin."

"Hey, sis. I can't believe you're holding out on me! Come on. Doesn't your favorite sister get to be among the first to hear?"

She tucked the phone in her shoulder and returned to

cutting the lemon for the marinade as she mentally reviewed her day for anything spill-worthy to her sister.

The store had been busy enough. She had busted the doddering and not-quite-right Mrs. Anglesey for trying to walk out of the store without paying for the pretty hand-beaded bracelet she tried on when she came into the store with her daughter.

But that sort of thing was a fairly regular occurrence whenever Beth and her mother came into the store and was handled easily enough, with flustered apologies from Beth and that baffled "what did I do wrong?" look from poor Mrs. Anglesey.

She didn't think Devin would be particularly interested in that or the great commission she'd earned by selling one of the beautiful carved horses an artist friend made in the woodshop behind his house to a tourist from Maine.

And then there was the pleasant encounter with Mr. Twitchell, but she doubted that was what her sister meant.

"Sorry. You lost me somewhere. I can't think of any news I have worth sharing."

"Seriously? You didn't think I would want to know that Ben Kilpatrick is back in town?"

The knife slipped from her hands and she narrowly avoided chopping the tip of her finger off. A greasy, angry ball formed in her stomach.

Ben Kilpatrick. The only person on earth she could honestly say she despised. She picked up the knife and stabbed it through the lemon, wishing it was his cold, black heart.

"You're joking," she said, though she couldn't imagine what her sister would find remotely funny about making up something so outlandish and horrible.

"True story," Devin assured her. "I heard it from Betty Orton while I was getting gas. Apparently he strolled into the grocery store a few hours ago, casual as a Sunday morning, and bought what looked to be at least a week's worth of groceries. She said he didn't look very happy to be back. He just frowned when she welcomed him back."

"It's a mistake. That's all. She mistook him for some-one else."

"That's what I said, but Betty assured me she's known him all his life and taught him in Sunday school three years in a row and she's not likely to mistake him for someone else."

"I won't believe it until I see him," she said. "He hates Haven Point. That's fairly obvious, since he's done his best to drive our town into the ground."

"Not actively," Devin, who tended to see the good in just about everyone, was quick to point out.

"What's the difference? By completely ignoring the property he inherited after his father died, he accomplished the same thing as if he'd walked up and down Lake Street, setting a torch to the whole downtown."

She picked up the knife and started chopping the fresh tarragon with quick, angry movements. "You know how hard it's been the last five years since he inherited to keep tenants in the downtown businesses. Haven Point is dying because of one person. Ben Kilpatrick."

If she had only one goal for her next four years as mayor, she dreamed of revitalizing a town whose lifeblood was seeping away, business by business.

When she was a girl, downtown Haven Point had been bustling with activity, a magnet for everyone in town, with several gift and clothing boutiques for both men and women, restaurants and cafés, even a downtown movie theater.

She still ached when she thought of it, when she looked around at all the empty storefronts and the ramshackle buildings with peeling paint and broken shutters.

"It's his fault we've lost so many businesses and nothing has moved in to replace them. I mean, why go to all the trouble to open a business," she demanded, "if the landlord is going to be completely unresponsive and won't fix even the most basic problems?"

"You don't have to sell it to me, Kenz. I know. I went to your campaign rallies, remember?"

"Right. Sorry." It was definitely one of her hot buttons. She loved Haven Point and hated seeing its decline—much like old Mrs. Anglesey, who had once been an elegant, respected, contributing member of the community and now could barely get around even with her daughter's help and didn't remember whether she had paid for items in the store.

"It wasn't really his fault, anyway. He hired an incompetent crook of a property manager who was supposed to be taking care of things. It wasn't Ben's fault the man embezzled from him and didn't do the necessary upkeep to maintain the buildings."

"Oh, come on. Ben Kilpatrick is the chief operating officer for one of the most successful, fastest-growing companies in the world. You think he didn't know what was going on? If he had bothered to care, he would have paid more attention."

This was an argument she and Devin had had before. "At some point, you're going to have to let go," her sister said calmly. "Ben doesn't own any part of Haven Point now. He sold everything to Aidan Caine last year—which makes his presence in town even more puzzling. Why would he come back *now*, after all these years? It would seem to me, he has even *less* reason to show his face in town now."

McKenzie still wasn't buying the rumor that Ben had actually returned. He had been gone since he was seventeen years old. He didn't even come back for Joe Kilpatrick's funeral five years earlier—though she, for one, wasn't super surprised about that since Joe had been a bastard to everyone in town and especially to his only surviving child.

"It doesn't make any sense. What possible reason would he have to come back now?"

"I don't know. Maybe he's here to make amends. Did you ever think of that?"

How could he ever make amends for what he had done to Haven Point—not to mention shattering all her girlish illusions?

Of course, she didn't mention that to Devin as she tossed the tarragon into the lemon juice while her sister continued speculating about Ben's motives for coming back to town.

Her sister probably had no idea about McKenzie's ridiculous crush on Ben, that when she was younger, she had foolishly considered him her ideal guy. Just thinking about it now made her cringe.

Yes, he had been gorgeous enough. Vivid blue eyes, long sooty eyelashes, the old clichéd chiseled jaw—not to mention that lock of sun-streaked brown hair that always seemed to be falling into his eyes, just begging for the right girl to push it back, like Belle did to the Prince after the Beast in her arms suddenly materialized into him.

Throw in that edge of pain she always sensed in him and his unending kindness and concern for his sickly younger sister and it was no wonder her thirteen-year-old self— best friends with that same sister—used to pine for him to notice her, despite the four-year difference in their ages.

It was so stupid, she didn't like admitting it, even to herself. All that had been an illusion, obviously. He might have been sweet and solicitous to Lily but that was his only redeeming quality. His actions these past five years had proved that, over and over.

Through the open kitchen window, she heard Rika start barking fiercely, probably at some poor hapless chipmunk or squirrel that dared venture into her territory.

"I'd better go," she said to Devin. "Rika's mad at something."

"Yeah, I've got to go, too. Looks like the Shelter Springs ambulance is on its way with a cardiac patient."

"Okay. Good luck. Go save a life."

Her sister was a dedicated, caring doctor at Lake Haven Hospital, as passionate about her patients as McKenzie was about their town.

"Let me know if you hear anything down at city hall about why Ben Kilpatrick has come back to our fair city after all these years."

"Sure. And then maybe you can tell me why you're so curious."

She could almost hear the shrug in Devin's voice. "Are you kidding me? It's not every day a gorgeous playboy billionaire comes to town."

And that was the crux of the matter. Somehow it seemed wholly unfair, a serious Karmic calamity, that he had done so well for himself after he left town. If she had her way, he would be living in the proverbial van down by the river—or at least in one of his own dilapidated buildings.

Rika barked again and McKenzie hurried to the back door that led onto her terrace. She really hoped it wasn't a skunk. They weren't uncommon in the area, especially not this time of year. Her dog had encountered one the week before on their morning run on a favorite mountain trail and it had taken her three baths in the magic solution she found on the internet before she could allow Rika back into the house.

Her dog wasn't in the yard, she saw immediately. Now that she was outside, she realized the barking was more excited and playful than upset. All the more reason to hope she wasn't trying to make nice with some odiferous little friend.

"Come," she called again. "Inside."

The dog bounded through a break in the bushes between the house next door, followed instantly by another dog—a beautiful German shepherd with classic markings.

She had been right. Rika *had* been making friends. She and the German shepherd looked tight as ticks, tails wagging as they raced exuberantly around the yard.

The dog must belong to the new renters of the Sloane house. Carol would pitch a royal fit if she knew they had a dog over there. McKenzie knew it was strictly prohibited.

Now what was she supposed to do?

A man suddenly walked through the gap in landscaping. He had brown hair, but a sudden piercing ray of the setting sun obscured his features more than that.

She *really* didn't want a confrontation with the man, especially not on a Friday night when she had been so looking forward to a relaxing night at home. She supposed she could just call Carole or the property management company and let them deal with the situation.

That seemed a cop-out since Carole had asked her to keep an eye on the place.

She forced a smile and approached the dog's owner. "Hi. Good evening. You must be renting the place from Carole. I'm McKenzie Shaw. I live next door. Rika, that dog you're playing catch with, is mine."

The man turned around and the pleasant evening around her seemed to go dark and still as she took in brown sun-streaked hair, steely blue eyes, chiseled jaw.

Her stomach dropped as if somebody had just picked her up and tossed her into the cold lake.

Ben Kilpatrick. Here. Staying in the house next door. So much for her lovely evening at home.

* * * * *

*Don't miss*
*REDEMPTION BAY by RaeAnne Thayne,*
*available July 2015 wherever*
*HQN Books are sold.*
*www.HQNBooks.com*

# COMING NEXT MONTH FROM

## HARLEQUIN®

# SPECIAL EDITION

## Available July 21, 2015

### #2419 Do You Take This Maverick?
*Montana Mavericks: What Happened at the Wedding?*
by Marie Ferrarella

Claire Strickland is in mommy mode, caring for her baby girl, Bekka. She doesn't have time for nights on the town...*unlike* her estranged husband, Levi Wyatt. The carousing cowboy wants to prove he's man enough to keep his family together, but can he show the woman he loves that their family is truly meant to be?

### #2420 One Night in Weaver...
*Return to the Double C* • by Allison Leigh

Psychologist Hayley Templeton has always pictured herself with an Ivy League boyfriend, but she can't seem to get sexy security guard Seth Banyon out of her mind. Overwhelmed with work, Hayley turns to Seth for relief in more ways than one. She soon finds there's more heart and passion to this seeming Average Joe than she ever could have imagined.

### #2421 The Boss, the Bride & the Baby
*Brighton Valley Cowboys* • by Judy Duarte

Billionaire Jason Rayburn is back home on his family's Texas ranch, looking to renovate and sell off the property. So he brings in lovely Juliana Bailey to help him clean up the Leaning R. Juliana is reluctant to work with irresistibly handsome Jason, who's the son of an infamous local businessman. Besides, she has a baby secret she's trying to keep—at the risk of her heart!

### #2422 The Cowboy's Secret Baby
*The Mommy Club* • by Karen Rose Smith

One night with bull rider Ty Conroy gave Marissa Lopez an amazing gift—her son, Jordan. She never expected to see the freewheeling cowboy again, but Ty is back in town after a career-ending injury forced him to start over. Both Marissa and Ty are reluctant to trust one another, but doing so might just lasso them the greatest prize of all—family!

### #2423 A Reunion and a Ring
*Proposals & Promises* • by Gina Wilkins

To ponder a proposal, Jenny Baer retreats to her childhood haunt, a cabin in the Arkansas hills. To her surprise, she's met there by her college sweetheart, ex-cop Gavin Locke. Years ago, their passion blazed brightly until Jenny convinced herself she wanted a more secure future. Can these long-lost lovers heal past wounds...and create the future together they'd always wanted?

### #2424 Following Doctor's Orders
*Texas Rescue* • by Caro Carson

Dr. Brooke Brown works tirelessly as an ER doctor. She does her best to ignore too-handsome playboy firefighter Zach Bisho, who threatens her concentration. But not even Brooke can resist, soon succumbing to his charm, and a fling soon turns into love...even as Zach discovers his adorable long-lost daughter. Despite past hurts, Brooke and Zach soon find that there's nowhere they'd rather be than in each other's arms...forever!

---

**YOU CAN FIND MORE INFORMATION ON UPCOMING HARLEQUIN® TITLES, FREE EXCERPTS AND MORE AT WWW.HARLEQUIN.COM.**

HSECNM0715

# REQUEST YOUR FREE BOOKS!
## 2 FREE NOVELS PLUS 2 FREE GIFTS!

**H HARLEQUIN®**

# SPECIAL EDITION
### Life, Love & Family

"You don't mind if I see her?" he asked uncertainly.

"No, I don't mind," Claire answered in the same quiet
voice. She gestured toward the baby lying in the portable
playpen. "Go on, it's okay. Since Bekka lights up whenever you walk into a room, maybe it might be a good
thing for her if you spent a little time with our little girl."

"Thanks," Levi said to her with feeling. Then he slanted
another look toward Claire—a longer one as he tried to
puzzle things out—and asked, "How do you feel about
my spending time with her mother?"

Claire arched one eyebrow as she regarded him. "I
wouldn't push it if I were you, Levi," she warned.

He raised his hands in a sign of complete surrender.
"Message received. You don't need to say another word,
Claire. My question is officially rescinded," he told her.

And then, because he prided himself on always being truthful with Claire, he added, "I'm a patient man. I can wait until you decide to change your mind about that."

Because he had really left her no recourse if she was to save face, Claire told him, "I don't think there's enough patience in the whole world for that."

"We'll see," Levi said softly, more to himself than to her. "We'll see."

Claire gave no indication that she had overheard him. But she had.

And something very deep inside her warmed to his words.

*Don't miss*
*DO YOU TAKE THIS MAVERICK?*
*by Marie Ferrarella, available August 2015 wherever*
*Harlequin® Special Edition books and ebooks are sold.*

www.Harlequin.com

**HARLEQUIN®**

A *Romance* FOR EVERY MOOD™

Stay up-to-date on all your
romance-reading news with the
*Harlequin Shopping Guide,*
featuring bestselling authors, exciting new
miniseries, books to watch and more!

The newest issue will be delivered right to you
with our compliments! There are 4 each year.

Signing up is easy.

## EMAIL

ShoppingGuide@Harlequin.ca

## WRITE TO US

HARLEQUIN BOOKS
Attention: Customer Service Department
P.O. Box 9057, Buffalo, NY 14269-9057

## OR PHONE

1-800-873-8635 in the United States
1-888-343-9777 in Canada

Please allow 4-6 weeks for delivery of the first issue by mail.

# THE WORLD IS BETTER WITH

*Romance*

Harlequin has everything from contemporary, passionate and heartwarming to suspenseful and inspirational stories.

## Whatever your mood, we have a romance just for you!

Connect with us to find your next great read, special offers and more.

f /HarlequinBooks

🐦 @HarlequinBooks

www.HarlequinBlog.com

www.Harlequin.com/Newsletters